BILLY SURE

·KID ENTREPRENEUR·

AND THE STINK SPECTACULAR

INVENTED BY **LUKE SHARPE**
DRAWINGS BY **GRAHAM ROSS**

Simon Spotlight

New York London Toronto Sydney New Delhi

SIMON SPOTLIGHT

An imprint of Simon & Schuster Children's Publishing Division

1230 Avenue of the Americas, New York, New York 10020

First Simon Spotlight hardcover edition May 2015

Copyright © 2015 by Simon & Schuster, Inc. Text by David Lewman. Illustrations by Graham Ross. All rights reserved, including the right of reproduction in whole or in part in any form.

SIMON SPOTLIGHT and colophon are registered trademarks of Simon & Schuster, Inc.

For information about special discounts for bulk purchases, please contact Simon & Schuster Special Sales at 1-866-506-1949 or business@simonandschuster.com.

Designed by Jay Colvin

The text of this book was set in Minya Nouvelle.

Manufactured in the United States of America 0415 FFG

10 9 8 7 6 5 4 3 2 1

ISBN 978-1-4814-3951-0 (hc)

ISBN 978-1-4814-3950-3 (pbk)

ISBN 978-1-4814-3952-7 (eBook)

Library of Congress Catalog Number 2014949479

Chapter One

Impostor Mom

I'M SITTING IN MY ROOM STARING AT MY LAPTOP. My brain feels like it's been zapped with a **FREEZE RAY**. I keep thinking the same thing over and over. Maybe my brain has been zapped with a repeat ray. Or a freeze and repeat ray.

How can this be?

How did this happen?

No way. NO WAY!

I read the e-mail from my mom for the twentieth time. Have I misunderstood?

No. There's really only one possible answer here.

My mom's e-mail clearly says that she

hasn't sent me any e-mails in weeks. And that she never switched to a new e-mail address. So for weeks I've been sending e-mails to someone *pretending* to be my mom. Not my real mom. A fake mom. An impostor mom!

And that's not good. It feels crummy. But it's even worse than that. I didn't just e-mail my mom with normal life updates—stuff like how the Hyenas are playing (that's our favorite baseball team, and they've been on a losing streak), or how annoying Emily has been (that's my sister, and for the record, that would be: *very* annoying). None of that would really matter. It'd be okay for Impostor Mom to know about that stuff. Some of it, like the fights with Emily, even our neighbors know about. So it's not exactly private information.

But I also wrote about my ideas for inventions. Which is bad. *Really* bad. Not to mention really private. Because, as you probably know by now, my inventions aren't just things I make up and draw on a piece of paper and then forget about. They're real products manufactured and sold by a real company, **SURE THINGS, INC.** (Named after me, Billy Sure, and run by me and my business partner and best friend, Manny.)

When I say "as you probably know by now," I'm not trying to brag or anything. It's just that our first two products, the ALL BALL ("The Only Ball You'll Ever Need!") and the SIBLING SILENCER ("Like A Mute Button For Your Brothers and Sisters!") are selling like crazy. And there have been lots of stories about Sure Things, Inc. on TV and the Internet. You probably even own an All Ball or a Sibling Silencer. (If your sibling owns a Sibling Silencer . . . um . . . sorry about that. Time to buy one of your own!)

So it's not a good idea for me to share my secret ideas about how to build my inventions with someone pretending to be my mom.

The question is, who is pretending to be my mom?

I've got to figure this out.

It's late at night and I'm sitting at my desk. I do some of my best thinking here . . . that is, when my brain isn't acting like it's been zapped by a freeze and repeat ray. My dog, Philo, is already asleep next to my bed. I can hear him breathing slowly, almost like he's snoring, but not quite. I kind of want to wake him up and tell him about my problem, but I know that won't do any good. It's not like he can tell me what to do.

Who is pretending to be my mom?!

It'd be nice to talk to someone about this. But I don't want to wake up my dad. And I *certainly* don't want to wake up Emily. That could prove fatal—I take my life in my hands walking into her room in broad daylight; I can't imagine that going into her room in the middle of the night would go over very well.

My mom's great to talk to, but she isn't here. She's off in Antarctica doing research for the government. Because of the storms down in Antarctica, the Internet's been down for weeks, so she hasn't been able to e-mail me. But I didn't know that. During those weeks, I was sending e-mails to IMPOSTOR MOM, blabbing about my new inventions like an idiot.

4

But it's not my fault, right? *I thought it was my mom!* Which brings me back to . . .

WHO IS PRETENDING TO BE MY MOM?!

Should I e-mail Manny? Manny is my best friend. He is also Sure Things, Inc.'s CFO (Chief Financial Officer), which means he keeps track of sales and the money. He's probably still up, checking the latest sales figures for the All Ball and the Sibling Silencer. But I'd hate to spoil his good mood. Right now he's really happy with the success of Sure Things, Inc.

And besides, I might get in serious trouble. Revealing secrets must have broken some company rule. Or maybe even the law! By sharing my ideas about new inventions, have I betrayed Sure Things, Inc., dooming our company to failure? Is Impostor Mom going to steal all my ideas and then take away our customers? What if Manny gets so mad at me that he refuses to forgive me? Only twelve years old, and already my life could be ruined.

This is serious.

I decide to lie in bed. I love my bed—it's warm and soft. I guess everyone loves their bed, right? I mean, you spend a lot of time there. It would be terrible to be stuck with a bed you hate. I wonder if you'd just start liking it after a while? Maybe it would become comfortable to you and you would forget that you ever hated it. And then if someone sits on your bed and says, "I hate this bed, it's so uncomfortable!" you'd get really mad and defend your bed because it's yours and you love it. I bet that's what happens.

I stare at the blueprints on my wall, lit up by the light from a streetlight outside my window. My dad framed the blueprints for the All Ball and the Sibling Silencer. Both sets

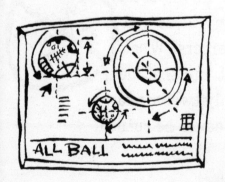

of blueprints were plans I drew up while I was sleep-inventing. I know it sounds weird, but sometimes, when I've been working on a new invention and I've gotten stuck, I get up in the night and finish the invention while I'm still asleep. For someone who loves his bed as much as I do, I still like to sleepwalk apparently. But it's not something I can turn off. I just do it. Plus, it's kind of a good thing because my sleepwalking has turned into sleep-inventing, and let's face it: Where would Sure Things, Inc. be without my inventions?

Speaking of Sure Things, Inc. . . . if it turns out that our company is ruined by my e-mails to Impostor Mom, will looking at those blueprints make me feel sad? If so, I'll definitely take them down and put up some posters. Maybe of Carl Bourette. He's the Hyenas shortstop, and my favorite baseball player.

Sleep is definitely out of the question. I get up and reread the e-mails I sent to Impostor Mom. I make myself read them with a "CRITICAL EYE." (My English teacher, Mrs. Boniface, taught us that term. At first I thought it meant that you could criticize everything you read, which was kind of fun, but what if you like the stuff you're reading? Manny doesn't have Mrs. Boniface, but he told me he thinks it means you're supposed to think really hard about stuff when you read it.) So after rereading my e-mails with a critical eye, I decide that maybe they're really not *that* bad. I didn't write anything all that specific about any new inventions. No details about how stuff works. I wrote more about baseball and school than I did about my inventions or Sure Things, Inc.

Philo twitches in his sleep, making funny sounds, like muffled barks. He must be dreaming. Maybe he's inventing something, like a gadget to let dogs open refrigerators. (There's an invention Sure Things, Inc. will *not* be making.) I get up out of my desk chair, walk over to his bed, kneel down, and pet him. Petting Philo always relaxes me.

I'm still not sure what to do about Impostor Mom, but I also do some of my best thinking when I'm asleep, so I should go back to bed. If I focus on how much I love my bed instead of worrying about Impostor Mom, eventually I will fall asleep. Right?

Maybe in the morning I'll know what to do.

I'm tied up in a chair. I struggle to escape, but the knots are way too tight. I look around for some kind of tool to cut the ropes, but I'm in a small empty room. There's nothing in here but me, the chair, and the ropes. I try to yell "HELP!" but somehow I can't make any sounds.

A tall man dressed all in gray enters. Gray hat. Gray suit. Gray shoes. Gray gloves. And a gray mask hiding his face. He stands still, with his hands hanging at his sides.

"Ready to talk?" he murmurs in a low, threatening voice.

"Talk about what?" I ask.

The man chuckles. "You may call me . . . Impostor Mom."

He walks over to the corner of the room. There's a table I didn't notice before. He picks up a small jar filled with liquid and a brush.

"Unless you talk," he says calmly, "I'm afraid I'm going to have to use more drastic measures."

I swallow hard. "Like what?"

"Like putting this ITCHING POWDER . . . ON YOUR NOSE!"

He dips the brush in the jar and moves toward me. I'm frozen. He begins to paint the itching powder onto my nose. . . .

LICK. LICK. LICK. . . .

I wake up from the nightmare and realize someone is licking my nose. Philo, of course. You might think that an inventor would invent a really cool alarm to wake himself up in the morning, but I don't need to. I've got a furry alarm that licks me awake every morning. Right on my nose.

"Okay, Philo, okay," I mumble. "Good morning. I'll get up."

I get up, and right away I remember what I was thinking about last night. What should I do about Impostor Mom?

I've got to talk to Manny. Even if it ruins his good mood. And even if what I've done could destroy our business forever. I've still got to tell him. We'll figure this out together. That's what best friends—and business partners—are for.

I get up and go to the bathroom. I'm ready to head downstairs to pour myself a bowl of cereal. Philo trots down the stairs ahead of me. It's Saturday, so I don't have to rush to school. But now that I've decided to tell Manny about Impostor Mom, I can't wait to get it over with. My stomach is growling, though, so I need to eat first.

But then I smell something that makes me lose my appetite. Something . . . AWFUL. I freeze on the second step.

Emily comes out of her bedroom. "Eww. What is that

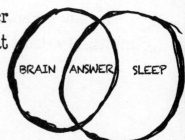

foul and horrid *smell*? Is it you, genius?"

Emily often calls me genius. But when she says it, it's not a compliment.

And she says it all with a British accent. But she's not British. Despite that little fact, she's been speaking with a British accent for the past few days. I have no idea why. But I have learned from experience with Emily that sometimes it's best not to ask why.

"It's not me," I say, heading downstairs again. "Maybe it's your accent. That stinks pretty bad."

"Wait!" she says. "Stop!"

I stop. I have no idea why she's telling me to stop. Is there a rattlesnake on the stairs? Nah, I think Philo would have noticed.

"I know what the horrid odor is," she says dramatically, as though she's announcing who the murderer is at the end of a mystery.

"What?"

"Dad's cooking breakfast!"

If she's right, this is a terrible develop-ment. My dad thinks he's a gourmet chef, but everything he makes is awful. Actually, awful is too kind a word to describe my dad's cooking. Maybe "disgusting beyond belief"? Philo won't even eat food my dad has cooked. And let me tell you, Philo lives for people-food. Just not people-food that's been cooked by my dad.

Luckily, my dad never makes breakfast because he's usually out painting in his studio in the backyard. He says he loves the early morning light.

Philo, Emily, and I cautiously make our way into the kitchen. Sure enough, Dad's at the stove, humming to himself as he turns something in a frying pan. Something **HISSES** and foul-smelling smoke wafts up from the pan.

"Dad?" Emily asks cautiously. "You're . . . making breakfast?" Even in a situation this upsetting, she doesn't lose her new accent.

"Good morning, honey!" he says cheerfully. "I sure am! Hungry?"

"But, Dad," I say, pointing to the window. "You're missing the beautiful morning light."

He salts whatever disgusting thing is in the

pan. "I am. And I still love the light right at sunrise. But for the paintings I'm doing right now, I prefer the light of sunset. So for the next couple of weeks, I can cook you breakfast!"

"Does this mean you won't be able to cook dinner?" Emily asks hopefully.

Dad laughs. "Of course not! Now, who wants turnip turnovers?"

He's holding a big sizzling green blob on the spatula. I'm not a turnip expert, but I'm pretty sure they're not usually green.

Emily and I start talking at the same time, firing off excuses one after the other. Here's what it sounds like in my kitchen:

"Sorry but . . . Ihavetoeatcerealforaspecial homeworkassignment–I'mallergictoturnips– onaturnipfreediet–fastingforworldpeace– Ialreadyatebreakfast . . . I HAVE TO GET TO THE OFFICE!" I finish loudly just as Emily pauses to take a breath.

I run out, knowing I will have to pay later for leaving Emily alone with my dad and his

turnip terrors . . . but when it comes to my dad's cooking, it's every kid for himself.

When I say I have to get to "the office," I'm telling the truth, because I really do have an office. The office of Sure Things, Inc. is in the garage at Manny's house. But it's not like any other office you've ever seen. Sure, there are desks and computers and office stuff like that, but there's much, much more.

We have: A soda machine that can make millions of flavors. A pizza machine that gives you a slice with whatever you want on it. (Now that I am outside in the fresh air, my appetite has miraculously reappeared. For breakfast, I think I'm going to have a slice with bananas and walnuts when I get to the office.) A baseball pitching machine. A foosball table. An air hockey table. Pretty much every video game console ever made. A pinball machine. And, of course, a punching bag.

And a basketball hoop. When I ride in the side door and lean my bike against the wall, Manny's standing at the free throw line he painted on the floor. Lately he's been trying to see how many free throws he can make in a row. He shoots an All Ball. *Swish!*

"Nine," he says, going to get the ball out of the trash can it's fallen into. "You know, I've been thinking about getting one of those chute things that you attach to the hoop so the ball comes right back to you. What do you think?"

"Sounds good," I say.

He walks over to his laptop and starts clicking his mouse through web pages. "Sweet. I'll order one right away."

"Yeah, but first I wanted to talk about something."

"Oh," he says, spinning in his chair to face me. "Okay, cool. What do you want to talk about? A new invention? It's really not too

soon to start thinking about our next product."

"No, it's not that," I say, picking up an All Ball and using the remote control to turn it into a tennis ball. I toss it up over the garage rafters and catch it. I'm not sure how to tell Manny about Impostor Mom. I sort of rehearsed in my head on the bike ride over, but then I started thinking about pizza and now I can't remember what I was going to say. "Um, you know my mom?"

"Of course," Manny says, looking at me strangely. "I've known your mom my entire life, Billy."

"Right," I say, nodding. "Well, while she's gone, in Antarctica, I've been writing her e-mails, you know?"

"Sure."

"But last night I got this e-mail from her saying the Wi-Fi's been down in Antarctica for the last few weeks."

"Probably on account of the storms," Manny says, shaking his head grimly.

Am I the only person in the world who

doesn't follow the weather in Antarctica?

"Yeah. Anyway, the thing is, I thought I was writing to my mom, but it turned out to be some impostor pretending to be my mom."

Manny's grim look gets even grimmer.

"What, you mean, like, a hacker?" he asks.

"I guess so," I say. "Whoever was pretending to be my mom got my e-mail address somehow and then lied and said my mom had a new e-mail address. I wrote back to that address."

Manny sees the problem right away. He looks very worried. The words start tumbling out of his mouth really fast. "What did you write about? Did you talk about your inventions? Did they *ask* about your inventions?"

I nod. Manny looks a little green. In fact, his skin tone reminds me of my dad's breakfast turnips. Now he looks like he's going to be sick . . . like he *ate* one of the breakfast turnips. My best friend is going to throw up and it's all my fault! I have to fix this!

I set the tennis ball down and hold my hands up for emphasis. "They asked a lot of questions, but I didn't talk about inventions that much! I reread all the e-mails last night with a critical eye, and I really don't think it's that bad."

Maybe it's my impressive use of the term "critical eye," but Manny looks calmer. His face goes from bright green to just slightly green. He gets up and starts pacing around. "CORPORATE ESPIONAGE! I suppose it had to happen sooner or later!"

"What do you mean?" I'm watching him pace, trying to figure out if he's going to throw up or not.

"You know, businesses spying on each other! I've read about it in my business journals! It happens all the time! I just didn't think it'd happen to us! At least not so soon. . . ."

He walks quickly over to the door, opens it, and looks around, checking for spies. "I should have seen this coming. I should have beefed up our security. When you're in the invention business, there are bound to be spies and thieves!" He closes the door and starts pacing across the room again, faster and faster.

A moment later he walks over to the pizza machine. "Want a slice?" he asks me, and I suddenly feel a thousand times better. It's not that bad if Manny wants pizza.

"Yeah, a slice with banana and walnuts," I say, grinning.

I walk over to where Manny is standing and watch him press buttons on the pizza maker. "Thanks for not freaking out," I tell him. "I know I messed up, and I'm sorry."

The pizza maker dings and a perfect slice of banana walnut pizza slides out. Manny slips a paper plate under the slice and hands it to me. "This isn't your fault, Billy," he says, and then he presses buttons on the pizza maker to create his own slice. Pepperoni-mushroom-sausage. "Let's eat and then we can figure this out," Manny adds just as his slice comes out. "We both think better on full stomachs."

Chapter Two

Real Mom

AFTER WE FINISH OUR PIZZA, MANNY MOTIONS TO the door leading into his house. I start to ask him why we're leaving the garage, when Manny raises a finger to his lips to SHUSH me. I raise my hands and eyebrows and make the universal sign and expression for "What?"

Manny grabs a pad and pen and scrawls a note that he holds up for me to see:

BEWARE OF BUGS!

Bugs? I quickly look around the garage but don't see any bugs.

Once inside the house, Manny drags me

into the kitchen. I'm starting to think he wasn't talking about the CREEPY-CRAWLY kind of bugs.

"Hi, Billy!" Manny's mom says as soon as she sees us. "How are things out in the office? You two need anything?"

"No, thanks, Mrs. Reyes," I say. "We're fine." I give Manny a pointed look. "Unless you want to ask your mom about bug spray?" I ask him.

Manny shakes his head and quickly reassures his mom that they don't have a bug problem in the garage. "What I meant is that we need to make sure the garage isn't bugged. You know, by the spies?" Manny's voice dips down to a whisper for the word "spies," as if maybe there are some hiding in the pantry and he doesn't want them to hear him talking about them.

Manny's mom watches our exchange and seems to decide she has nothing to worry about as long there's not an insect infestation in her garage. "You don't have to call me 'Mrs. Reyes,' Billy," she says. "You can call me DR. REYES!" She laughs. This is her favorite joke.

Manny's parents are always really nice to me. Emily says of course they're nice—their son is super rich because of my inventions. But she's wrong about that. First of all, I've known Manny since first grade, and his parents have *always* been nice to me. One time I threw up all over the fancy blue rug in their living room after Manny and I pigged out on Halloween candy, and Mrs. Reyes—sorry, Dr. Reyes—didn't get mad at all. And second, neither of us is super rich yet. I mean, maybe on paper. But most of the money goes right back into Sure Things, Inc. That's how it is with a new company. Our parents handle the money that comes to us, putting most of it in the bank for college. And then there's the fact that none of my inventions would have ever amounted to anything without Manny. There would be no Sure Things, Inc. without my CFO. So, as usual, Emily has no idea what she's talking about.

After chatting with Manny's mom, we head up to his bedroom. There are three chessboards with the pieces set up on them. Manny loves chess. He says chess is a lot like the business world—strategy and tactics and moves and countermoves. And he's really good at it. I don't know if he's like a grandmaster, but I do know he beats me every time, usually in about five minutes. I don't play chess with Manny anymore.

The nightstand by his bed is covered with a stack of business journals. I don't know how he reads that stuff. I flipped through one of them once and got so bored I actually preferred talking to Emily.

He opens his closet. It's nothing like mine. His is neat and organized, with everything carefully placed on shelves and in bins. Mine is like a pile of clothes and junk with a door to keep it from EXPLODING into my room.

Manny reaches into the closet and pulls out an old beige computer. "The power cord should be here somewhere," he says, opening a plastic box with neatly coiled cords. Each one is labeled to show which device it goes with. I wasn't kidding when I said he was organized.

"Are you sure there's a power cord?" I say. "Maybe we're supposed to crank it. Or maybe it runs on steam."

"You're joking, but a hand-crank computer for people without electricity is actually a pretty good idea," he says, making a quick note on a pad of paper. Manny is always jotting down ideas and then bringing them up to me later. It's a good thing he does that, because I forget half that stuff I say two seconds after the words come out of my mouth.

He plugs the computer in and turns it on.

"So that antique actually works," I say. "But will it even connect to the Internet?"

"It's not *that* old!" Manny insists. "And most importantly, it's perfect for a secure conversation. It's old enough that the new malware programs probably won't even work on it. But video chat should."

Manny sits at his desk. I sit next to him in a chair I've pulled up. We watch the screen slowly light up. "Do you know which research facility your mom is stationed at?" he asks as he drums his fingers next to the keyboard, waiting for the screen to fully come up.

"Um, no, she's never mentioned the name of the facility," I tell him. "Maybe it's a secret."

Manny turns and looks at me. "So your mother travels the world doing research for the government, and her exact location might be a secret. Has it ever occurred to you that she might be a SPY?"

I laugh. "My mom? A spy?"

Manny clicks the mouse and types on the keys, setting up the computer for video chat. "Yeah! Does she ever tell you any of the details of what she's researching?"

I think about it. Sometimes Mom brings me souvenirs from the countries she visits, but I can't really remember her ever telling me anything specific about the work she does. Unless she's told me, and I forgot? It's not that

I don't listen to my mom, but sometimes I tune out boring stuff. It's very possible she told me and it was boring grown-up stuff and I can't remember any of it.

Could Manny be right? Is my mom a spy?

"No," I say. "But maybe that's just normal. Does your mom tell you about the specifics of her work?"

Manny laughs. "My mom's a podiatrist! Dad and I don't *let* her talk about the specifics of her work, especially at dinner! Do you have any idea how many GROSS FOOT DISEASES there are?"

I think about that for a moment and immediately see his point. "I'm guessing *all* foot diseases are gross."

"Exactly."

Manny slides over, and I use the keyboard to e-mail my mom, telling her we need to video chat about something important. I make sure I send this to her real e-mail address, not the fake address Impostor Mom told me to send my e-mails to.

Now we just have to wait for her reply.

"So," Manny says, "while we're waiting, I wanted to talk to you about a suggestion we got for expanding the Sibling Silencer line."

"What is it?"

"A few parents have requested that we make a Son Silencer. You know, a device that parents could use on their sons."

"We can't do that!"

"I agree."

"I guess maybe a Daughter Silencer might be all right . . . ," I say, imagining what it would be like to give each of my parents a Daughter Silencer for Christmas. Best. Gift. Ever.

"Yeah," Manny agrees. "But then if we didn't make a SON SILENCER, people would say we're being unfair."

I think about that for a moment. As usual, Manny is right. "Well, there's no way we're making a Son Silencer!"

"Right," Manny says. "So I guess we'll just leave the Sibling Silencer the way it is, and not expand that line. It's too bad, because the product's doing great."

PING BONG BING! An electronic song plays on the old computer. My mom's calling on video chat! I click on "Answer With Video" and suddenly there she is.

"Hi, honey," she says. "Everything all right?"

"Hi, Mom! Everything's fine. Sort of. I'm here with Manny." I don't want her to say anything too mushy in front of my friend.

"Hi, Carol," Manny says, leaning in so the camera can pick him up. My parents have encouraged Manny to call them by their first names. At first I could tell he felt awkward doing it, but now he seems to have gotten used to it. It still sounds kind of weird to me.

I notice that Mom's dressed all in black, and that she's got some kind of harness attached to her. "Are you . . . busy?" I ask. "Doing something? That requires a harness?"

She glances at the harness and shrugs. "What I was doing can wait," she says. "I want to know what's going on with you."

I start to tell her about Impostor Mom, but Manny interrupts. "Before we start, is this line secure on your end?"

Mom raises her eyebrows and then smiles. "Oh, yes. Very secure."

"For your spy work?" Manny blurts out.

Mom's smile falters for a moment, and then she laughs. "For my research," she says firmly.

See? I knew my mom wasn't a spy!

I bring Mom up to date on what happened with my e-mail. I tell her all about Impostor Mom, and how Manny and I are worried that our office might be bugged. "So *that's* why I didn't get more e-mails from you," she says. "When the Wi-Fi came back on, I thought I'd find all these e-mails from you. But I didn't."

I feel bad about that, even though it wasn't my fault. "I'm sorry, Mom. I was writing e-mails to you. But I was sending them to the wrong address."

She nods. "I understand. Don't worry about that. I just wanted you to know how much I look forward to your e-mails." She smiles a big, warm smile, and I feel better right away.

"Now," she says, getting down to business, "about these e-mails you sent to this Impostor Mom. Did the impostor ask you anything about my work?"

I shake my head. "No, because the impostor was pretending to *be* you, so he or she wouldn't *ask* about you."

"I know," she says. "I just have to make sure. Did the impostor ask about OPERATION TIGER TOOTH?"

Operation Tiger Tooth? I try to ignore the look Manny is shooting me. The one that says, *Why is your mom asking you about Operation Tiger Tooth if she's not a spy?*

"No," I say, trying to act as if this were a perfectly normal thing to talk about with your mom. "They didn't mention Operation Tiger Tooth."

"Or PROJECT CENTAURI?"

I just shake my head. I catch another glimpse of Manny, and his eyes have gotten really big behind his glasses.

Mom looks reassured. "Okay," she says. "Take me through what they *did* ask about."

I tell her about how Impostor Mom asked about my inventions in pretty much every single e-mail.

Mom sighs. "I'm afraid it's clear what's going on here."

"Corporate espionage?" Manny asks.

"Yes," Mom confirms. "A spy from a rival business is definitely trying to learn your secrets. The good news is, I don't think you have to worry about your office being bugged—I think your spy has used e-mail infiltration. The bad news is, I think your spy has used e-mail infiltration!"

WORST-CASE SCENARIO: CONFIRMED!

"I knew it!" Manny says. He actually sounds happy. He loves being right. But this is not a happy piece of news. I've definitely been trading e-mails with a spy. This is so not good.

"So what do we do now?" I ask.

My mom knits her eyebrows together the way she does when she's thinking really hard. "I have some resources at my disposal that might be helpful," she says.

"What kind of resources does a 'researcher' in Antarctica have?" Manny asks.

"You don't need to know the details," my mom replies. She's sounding more like a spy by the minute. "In the meantime, you should keep writing e-mails to the corporate spy."

"*What?* I don't want to ever write to that fake again! I was planning to delete the impostor from my contacts list and block all communications from that e-mail address."

Mom shakes her head. "That's no way to catch a spy. You have to keep the lines of communication going. You can't let the spy know that you know he or she is a spy."

"That makes sense," Manny says, nodding his head. "If you stop writing to spies, they'll know you're onto them."

"So what?" I ask. "Isn't the whole point to stop communicating so the spy can't learn our secrets?"

"Yeah," Manny says. "You want to be sure you don't reveal any secrets. But we also want to find out who the spy is."

"Exactly," Mom says. "You two need to launch your own investigation."

Manny and I look at each other nervously. He knows business, and I know invention, but we're not spies. How do you spy on a spy?

Mom sees our nervous looks. She tries to reassure us. "You can do this, Billy. I'm going to e-mail you a special software program that will provide you with the identity of anyone who e-mails you—their *real* identity, not their fake one!"

"So we'll know the spy's real name?" Manny asks, excited.

"Not just the name," Mom says, leaning forward as if she's getting really into this. "With this program, you get a picture of the person who sent you the e-mail."

"That's amazing!" I cry. "How does it work?"

"I'm afraid I can't tell you," Mom says. "It's top secret."

Manny shoots me another look. I know what he's thinking: *Top secret?! That's spy talk!*

"In fact," Mom continues, "the copy of the software program I'm sending you will only work for five days. Then it will self-destruct."

Another quick look from Manny. *Self-destruct?! That's DEFINITELY spy talk!*

"Got it," I say. "So we've got to get the spy to write back to me within five days."

"Basically, we need to set a trap," Manny says. "An e-mail trap!"

"Exactly!" Mom exclaims, grinning happily that Manny caught on so quickly.

A trap? Well, that does sound interesting. . . .

Chapter Three

To Catch a Spy

AFTER I SAY GOOD-BYE TO MOM, MANNY SHUTS down his antique computer. "Let's go back to the office now that we know we don't have to worry about bugs," he says. "I think better there. Plus, there's pizza."

Back in the office, Manny heads straight to the pizza machine and starts picking his toppings for his second slice of pizza that morning: green pepper, olive, red onion, basil. He actually likes vegetables—it's weird.

When his slice is ready, he takes a bite, but then sets it back down on the paper plate and

picks up the large All Ball. It's still in basketball mode. He walks over to the free throw line, bounces the ball a couple of times, and pushes the ball from his chest.
SWISH!

"One," he counts. "So, we've got the secret software from your mom, the spy. . . ."

"She's not a spy!"

"Oh, she's a spy all right."

"We don't actually know that. Don't jump to conclusions. Research scientists have to keep their work secret too."

He gets the ball out of the trash can, walks back to the free throw line, and shoots again.
SWISH!

"Two. Why would a research scientist need software that secretly takes a picture of whoever's sending them e-mails?"

"I don't know," I say. "Maybe sometimes scientists try to steal ideas, so they use software to learn who the thieves are."

Manny raises his eyebrows skeptically. I know he's sticking with this spy business because he thinks it's cool, but it's kind of freaking me out. I mean, it's weird to think that your mom might have a secret job. A secret dangerous job.

"Look, can we deal with the real spy, Impostor Mom, first?" I say finally. "One spy in my life is enough right now."

And just like that, Manny drops it. "You're right. Let's think about Impostor Mom and the trap we're going to set." **SWISH!** "Three," he adds a moment later.

Do I have a great best friend or what?

I walk over to the air hockey table and slide a puck across it. "Okay, so let's focus. How are we going to trap this corporate spy?"

Manny tosses up another free throw. **SWISH!** "Well, your mom said you should get Impostor Mom to write back so we can use the spy software to identify him or her."

I nod. "But what should I write?"

"Something that'll definitely get Impostor Mom to write you back."

"How about: Help! I just accidentally fell

into a hole and I don't know what to do! E-mail me back ASAP with advice to save me!"

Manny makes a confused face. "You fell in a hole with your computer?"

"I could be writing on my phone. Impostor Mom would have to write back—I mean, what mom wouldn't want to help her kid if he fell into a hole?"

I'm really liking this plan. Until Manny points out the obvious.

"If you have a phone, why don't you just call your dad? Or nine-one-one?"

Reason #478 why I chose Manny to be my CFO: He has a lot of common sense.

Manny takes another free throw. This one bounces just off the rim. He doesn't seem to notice. "Impostor Mom is a corporate spy, right?" he asks, getting up from his chair.

"Right," I say.

"So what the spy wants to know about is your latest invention."

"Yeah, exactly. But I can't give away our company secrets. That'll ruin everything!"

Manny shoots another basket from behind the air hockey table. It's a shot I've seen him make a million times. **CLUNK!** The ball bounces off the rim again. It almost hits the soda machine, but Manny manages to catch it in time. "But what if you tell Impostor Mom about an invention we're *not* doing? That could be the bait in our trap!"

That sounds good to me. We talk about some of the inventions we've been mulling over recently. A **PERSONAL FORCE FIELD BELT**: You put on the belt, press a button, and you've got a force field around you that no one can get through. Objects couldn't get through, either. With a Personal Force Field Belt, you could make sure you were never hit with a water balloon again. Guaranteed protection against wedgies, noogies, wet willies, and more.

PERSONAL
FORCE FIELD
BELT

Or the **DOG TRANSLATOR**. It'd be so great to know what your dog was saying every time he barked. I'd love to know exactly what Philo is trying to say. (Most of the time, it's probably "Give me more treats, please!") I'm sure the millions of people who own dogs would all want a Dog Translator. I guess we could try to make a Cat Translator, too, but I'm personally more interested in hearing what dogs have to say. Cats would probably just complain about dogs. And everything. I don't know why, but cats seem like big complainers.

The **3-D CHOCOLATE PRINTER**. This would be so great. Not only could you print a three-dimensional object, you could print it in chocolate! Then you could eat it! It'd be like printing your own candy bars. Only they wouldn't have to be bars—they could be lizards or shoes or even little statues of you! (Though I'm not sure why you'd want to eat a chocolate statue of yourself. So you could pretend to be a giant? A giant who is eating you? Why would you possibly want to do that?)

There's nothing I love more than talking about inventions, but there's a problem.

"These are all *good* ideas," I say. "What we need is a *bad* idea."

"We do?" Manny asks, puzzled.

"Sure! We don't want to give away a good idea to Impostor Mom. We want to keep all our good ideas to ourselves. What we need is a bad idea that we don't care about giving away."

Manny nods. "That makes sense. The idea would have to be bad enough that we don't want to invent it, but *interesting* enough for Impostor Mom to write back asking for more details."

Manny quickly walks over to our dry-erase board. He uncaps a purple marker and writes "BAD" and "INTERESTING" on the board.

We both stare at the board, thinking.

"A TURTLE TRANSLATOR?" I suggest.

"Why is that a bad idea?"

"Who cares what turtles think?"

"Other turtles. Turtle owners. Fishermen."

"Why do fishermen care what turtles think?"

"You could send the turtle into the water to find out where the fish are, and then the turtle could report back to you," Manny says. "Turtle Translator is an excellent idea. I'm writing it down." He makes a note on his phone.

I get an idea. "Maybe we should look for ideas on the website! It's full of bad ideas!"

We've got this website called Sure Things' Next Big Thing where kids from all over the world can send in their ideas for inventions. If an idea's really good, we help make the product and share the money with the inventor. That's where the Sibling Silencer came from. A girl named Abby came up with the idea and a rough prototype, and then Sure Things, Inc. turned it into a successful product. (Again, I apologize if your brother or sister has one.)

I turn to my laptop, click on the website, type in my username and password, and scroll through kids' ideas. "Let's see . . . the SOAP SCUM ELIMINATOR, the LEAF-CATCHING TREE SKIRT (so you never have to rake leaves again), the TIME TRAVEL MACHINE-boy,

Manny, we sure do get that one a lot."

"Because it's a great idea," Manny says. "It's just very, very hard to invent."

"Like, maybe, impossible," I say, staring at the screen. Then I spin around in my chair. "This doesn't feel right. Looking at these kids' ideas and using them as Impostor Mom bait. Sure, a lot of these ideas are pretty bad, but the kids like them. It seems mean somehow to use them as bad ideas."

"But you just said they were bad ideas!"

"I know, but there's a difference between just saying, 'Oh, that's a bad idea,' and ignoring it, and saying, 'Oh, that's a bad idea, so I think I'll use it as bait to catch Impostor Mom.'"

"The kids will never even know we did it!"

"Are you sure?" I ask. "What if Impostor Mom *really* takes the bait and runs with the bad idea and manufactures it! Then the kid who came up with the idea would see that we gave it to a mean manufacturer who steals ideas!"

Manny thinks about this and nods. "Yeah,

I see what you mean. It's just not right. We'll have to come up with a bad idea of our own."

"That shouldn't be too hard," I say.

Actually, it is.

We need an original bad idea of our own that the spy will go for. We have to make sure it's not *so* bad that it'll give away the fact that we're onto the spy. If the spy smells a trap, whoever it is might refuse to answer our e-mail and cut off communication. We'll never find out who Impostor Mom is. And never get revenge.

We come up with a few ideas, but none of them seem right. Manny can still see something good about them. He writes them down and refuses to let us tell the spy about them.

Manny and I decide to sleep on it. There's no rush.

Except that Mom's secret software will self-destruct in five days . . .

At school on Monday I'm still thinking about the perfect bad idea. I haven't come up with anything when lunchtime rolls around, so I decide to sit by myself. Manny is cool with it. He knows that I need to concentrate. Maybe I'll think of something while I'm eating.

I chew my sandwich and look around. A small kid named Jacob has a can of Dr. Fizzy soda to drink with his lunch. He must have brought it from home, because the cafeteria definitely doesn't sell Dr. Fizzy. They probably should, though, because it's popular.

Unfortunately, another kid sees Jacob's soda too: Darrell Fliborg. If bullies had a club, Darrell would be president.

"Hey," Darrell says to Jacob. "Where'd you get that?"

"Get what?" Jacob asks nervously. Conversations with Darrell Fliborg rarely end well, and he knows it. Jacob's smart.

"That can of Dr. Fizzy," Darrell grunts.

"Oh," Jacob says, sensing trouble. "I, uh, brought it from home."

Darrell smiles, but it's not a friendly smile. More of a "just

what I wanted to hear" kind of smile. "Then I'm afraid I'm gonna have to conjugate it. No outside drinks allowed."

Knowing what's good for him, Jacob doesn't correct Darrell's use of "conjugate" by telling him he means "confiscate." But he does do something interesting.

Though he keeps looking right at Darrell, I see Jacob sneak his hand over to his sandwich. There's a red onion sticking out of the sandwich. Jacob rubs the red onion between his fingers.

"Oh," Jacob says, stalling for time, "I didn't know that. Well, that's okay. I think there might be something wrong with this can of Dr. Fizzy anyway."

Darrell squints suspiciously. "What's wrong with it?"

"I don't know," Jacob says. "It just smells really weird. Here."

Jacob holds the can right under Darrell's nose. What Darrell doesn't realize is that he's also holding his FINGERS right under Darrell's nose—the same fingers he used to rub the onion!

"EW!" Darrell says loudly, pulling his head back. "Gross! Get that away from me!" He leaves to go find someone else to bully. Unfortunately, there's always someone else.

As he leaves, Jacob smiles and wipes his fingers on a napkin. Then he takes a good, long drink from his can of Dr. Fizzy. Even though he wiped his fingers, he holds the can close to its base. Onion smell is hard to remove.

Jacob's little trick is brilliant. And it gives me an idea. . . .

After school I pick up Philo at my house. (He's thrilled to see me, but then he's *always* thrilled to

see me—and just about everyone else, too. Maybe not the mail carrier or the veterinarian, but pretty much everyone else.) We head on over to the office together. I'm eager to tell Manny my idea.

When we get there, Manny's standing at the free throw line. Once again, he's holding the large All Ball in its basketball form. Since Manny got on his free throw kick, I don't think it's been changed to any of the other four forms (soccer, foot, volley, or bowling ball).

"Twenty," he says when we walk in.

"Twenty free throws in a row? That's great!"

"No," he explains. "Twenty is my *goal*. So far I've got six in a row."

I unclip Philo from his leash and he goes straight to the water bowl we keep for him in the office. **SHLURP! SHLURP! SHLURP!**

"Why have a goal of twenty?" I ask. "Would you really stop if you made twenty free throws in a row? Why not have a goal of infinity?" ∞

"Because setting realistic goals is one of the secrets to success," Manny says. "All the business books say so."

49

"Okay," I say, launching a ball in the pin-ball machine. "Then maybe your goal should be seven. Not twenty."

"Ha-ha," Manny says. He throws the ball. *Clunk!* "That's your fault. You threw me off."

"No, you threw the *ball* off. *Way* off." The pinball rolls straight down between my flip-pers. I flap the flippers like mad, but it's no use. I turn away from the pinball machine. "I have an idea."

"What is it?" Manny asks. He sits down and looks right at me. When I say I have an idea, he always gives me his full attention.

"It's called the STINK SPECTACULAR," I say.

"Okay . . . ," Manny says doubtfully.

"It's a drink, obviously, that smells terrible, but tastes great."

Manny still looks confused. "Why?"

"So that you'll want to drink it. You wouldn't want to drink it if it didn't taste good."

"No, I mean why does it smell terrible?"

"I'm glad you asked. The terrible smell

makes the drink bully-proof! Let's say a bully starts to steal your delicious soda. He takes one little whiff, and *zoom!* That bully's out of there! He leaves, and you get to enjoy your delicious Stink Spectacular!"

Manny just sits there for a second, thinking about this. Then he smiles. "Oh! I get it! This is your *bad* idea! To use as bait for the spy!"

This hurts my feelings a little bit. I don't think the Stink Spectacular is a bad idea. I think it's a *great* idea!

"No!" I argue. "This isn't a bad idea! It's a really good idea! I think it should be Sure Things, Inc.'s next product!"

"Seriously?" Manny asks.

"Yes! Seriously!"

"Nobody wants to drink a drink that smells terrible," he argues. "Isn't smell, like, some huge percentage of taste, anyway? How can something smell terrible and taste great?"

"I don't know," I say, picking up a small All Ball and tossing it in the air. "How can one ball change into five balls? I didn't used to know that, either, but I figured it out."

I keep tossing the ball and catching it. Normally Manny would use the remote control to change the ball while it was in the air, but he doesn't do it this time. He just sits there, thinking.

"How often do bullies try to steal your drink?" Manny asks. "Is that really a common problem?"

"I don't know—look it up," I suggest.

"What am I searching for?" he asks. "'Bully steals drinks?'"

"Sure," I say. He hits the keys on his laptop. We're both quiet for a while.

"You know, though," I finally say, "there might be a *version* of the Stink Spectacular that could work as bait for the spy. . . ."

Chapter Four

Stench Quench

WE'RE BACK IN MANNY'S BEDROOM. I'M TYPING ON his antique computer. When I work on this thing, I feel as though I should be wearing a top hat and a black suit. I tell Manny this.

"You mean like you should be dressed formally?" he asks, confused.

"No, I should be dressed like in olden times, because it's an antique."

"I think people still wear top hats and black suits to really formal occasions."

"Like what?"

"Presidential inaugurations?"

I look at what I've written to Impostor Mom.

Dear Mom,
    Hi! How are you doing? I'm fine, and so is Philo. And Emily. And Dad.

"Seems kind of stiff," Manny says. "Is this the way you always write to your mom?"

"Yeah," I lie. Then I admit the truth. "No, not really. But I'm kind of nervous. I mean, I know I'm writing to a corporate spy, not my mom. It's weird. It's also kind of strange writing with you reading over my shoulder."

"Sorry, but this is important Sure Things, Inc. business," Manny says, sitting back a little. "Just pretend you're writing to your mom. But don't give away any of our real secrets."

"Duh," I say, deleting what I've written.
I start over.

Hi, Mom,
    Everyone here is great. We sure do miss you. When will you be back home?

"That's better," Manny says. "But you'd better cut that last question."

"Why?" I ask. "That's exactly what I'd say to my mom!"

"Yeah, but it might freak out Impostor Mom, since he or she doesn't know the real answer."

That is actually a pretty good point. I hit the backspace key. Then I resume typing.

School is good. Yesterday I found out I got an A on that math test.

Emily's still speaking in a British accent. She even calls the hood of the car the "bonnet" and the elevator the "lift."

Dad's working on a series of paintings lit by the sunset instead of the sunrise, which means he's been fixing us breakfast. Today he made pancakes with celery, fennel, liver, and lingonberries.

I taught Philo a new trick. It's called Lying Around Doing Nothing. He's—not surprisingly—really good at it.

"Okay, now it seems like you're stalling."

"This is exactly the kind of stuff I write to my mom! Isn't that what you want me to do?!"

"I do! But the parts about your family and dog don't have to be long. Impostor Mom's probably going to skip those parts anyway!"

"Okay, fine. Let's bait the trap. . . ."

Things at Sure Things, Inc. are great. The All Ball and the Sibling Silencer are selling really well. Manny's thrilled with our sales.

"You're putting *me* in this?!"

"Yeah, I have to if I'm going to talk about the business! Which is kinda the whole point!"

Manny frowns. "I don't know if I like having a corporate spy know my name."

"Your name is already very well known as part of Sure Things, Inc.! It'd take, like, two seconds to search 'Sure Things' and have your name pop up!"

"Yeah, well, I still don't like it."

"Now you know how I feel. You don't like having your name mentioned. *I've* got to write to the spy and pretend it's my mom!"

"Just go ahead and write."

Even though our first two products are doing great, Manny says it's really important to get another product going right away.

"Oh, so now you're going to put my name in every single sentence. Nice."

I laugh.

We've been kicking around ideas, and we've come up with one that we really like.

"That's the fourth time you've used 'really.'"

"It's an e-mail to my mom! Not an English assignment! Do *you* want to write it?"

Manny considers it. Then he shakes his head. "No, you know how you've been writing to the spy? This has to sound like your other e-mails. If all of a sudden this e-mail sounds different, Impostor Mom might get suspicious. Go on."

This is definitely a million-dollar idea! It's called Stench Quench. It's a drink that smells terrible . . . and tastes even worse! Kids are gonna love it. There's nothing kids love more than being grossed out, according to Manny's marketing magazines. I'm working on the formula, trying to get the stench just right. I'm so excited about this idea!

"I was going to put 'really excited,' but I changed it in your honor," I say.
"Thanks. 'Preciate it."

Well, I hope you're doing great. I'd write more, but I want to get back to work on my secret formula for Stench Quench.
Love, Billy

"Do you think maybe 'secret formula' is pushing it a little too much?" Manny asks.

"No, not at all. Everyone wants to know the 'secret formula.' That makes the bait even more . . . baity."

I read over what I've written. I put the cursor over the send button, but I hesitate. "Okay," I say. "Last chance to not communicate with a corporate spy. Are we sure we want to do this?"

Manny takes a big breath and lets it out. "Yeah. Send it."

CLICK!

And off it goes! My first e-mail to a corporate spy! No, wait—that's wrong. I've written a bunch of e-mails to this spy. I just didn't know I was writing to a spy. This is my first e-mail *deliberately* written to a corporate spy.

"I'm not sure about this," Manny says, looking worried.

"Oh, *now* you're not sure about this?! After I've already sent the e-mail? Great!"

"Sorry! I'm just . . . not sure."

"What are you not sure about?"

"STENCH QUENCH."

"What about it?" I get up and wander around

Manny's room. I consider moving some of the pieces on the chessboards without Manny seeing, but that seems mean. Funny, but mean. I'm pretty sure these are games he's playing with people over the Internet or something.

"It's just so . . . weird! A drink that smells and tastes terrible? I'm afraid Impostor Mom may not go for it. Or even worse—the spy may smell the stink of bait and never write to you again."

"It's not *that* weird. Kids do like gross stuff. That part is true. In second grade, Mike Stevenson showed me his booger collection. He had them taped to the pages of a notebook, with labels and everything."

"What did the labels say? 'BIG BOOGER?' 'LITTLE BOOGER?'"

"I don't remember. I think they had dates."

"Of what?"

"I'm not sure. The picking?"

"Okay, well, that's different from Stench Quench. Mike Stevenson wasn't drinking or eating boogers."

"Actually, I'm pretty sure he was."

"Gross!"

I stare at the computer screen. "I wonder how long it'll take for Impostor Mom to write back."

"*If* Impostor Mom writes back," Manny says.

We both sit there, staring at the screen together. "Let's talk about the Stink Spectacular a little bit," I suggest.

"Speaking of gross ideas," Manny replies.

"It's not a gross idea!" I protest. "I mean, yeah, it'll *smell* gross! But it'll taste great! Millions of kids are sure to buy it! Think of the 'gross' profits!"

Manny doesn't laugh at my pun. "I don't know, Billy," he says. "I'm still just not sure about this idea. I think you should keep thinking about what our next product should be.

Maybe take a look at some of the Sure Things'
Next Big Thing ideas."

"I don't need to look at the website! *This* is
our next big thing! I'm sure of it!"

Manny lets out a big breath.

Then . . . **DING!**

A new e-mail!

We both lean forward to see who it's from.
Impostor Mom!

Manny and I both try to grab the mouse to
click on the e-mail. He wins.

Hi, honey,

Now that I know it's some corporate spy
writing to me, I find the "Hi, honey" greeting
really disturbing.

Thanks for writing back to me. You must
be awfully busy with work—I haven't heard
much from you lately! But I understand that
your company and your schoolwork take
most of your time.

"Laying on the guilt," Manny says. "Pretty good at pretending to be a mom."

Speaking of your work, I'm so glad you and Manny are coming up with new ideas!
Not quite sure I understand the idea of Stench Quench, though. Why would kids want to buy a drink that smells terrible?

"I agree with you, Impostor Mom!" Manny yells.

Maybe you can explain the whole thing to me. Feel free to send me details.

"Okay," Manny says, taking a deep breath. "Time for the big question. Did your mom's super-secret spy software work?"

"Let's see," I say. I click on the e-mail and drag it over to the icon for the software my mom sent me. The software goes to work. . . .

"Is there a name?" Manny asks eagerly. "And a picture?"

"There sure is."

"Who is it?"

"Some yucky-looking guy with stringy gray hair and an enormous . . . is that a wart? . . . on his forehead."

"That sounds like Alistair Swiped!" Manny exclaims.

I have no idea who Alistair Swiped is, so Manny explains that he's the head of one of our biggest rival companies, Swiped Stuff, Inc. Manny, of course, knows all about him because, as CFO, it's his job to know stuff like that. He's really good at his job.

"Is he in his underwear?" Manny asks, squinting at the picture.

"No," I say. "But he's picking his nose."

"Maybe he'll send his boogers to Mike Stevenson."

"I think Mike moved on to collecting baseball cards. At least, I *hope* he did."

Manny leans back in his chair, puts his hands behind his head, and looks up at the ceiling of his bedroom. "So the corporate spy

is Alistair Swiped. I guess that makes perfect sense, in light of the EVERY BALL."

That's right! I forgot about the Every Ball! Swiped Stuff, Inc. came out with the Every Ball, an obvious rip-off of our All Ball a few months after our All Ball hit the market. It costs a little less than the All Ball, so some kids bought it thinking they were getting a cheaper version of the All Ball, but then word quickly spread that the Every Ball was just a golf ball zipped inside a baseball. And a crummy golf ball at that. And a lousy zipper. Soon the Every Ball was off the store shelves. We thought that Swiped Stuff, Inc. had gone out of business.

Apparently we were wrong.

When I think about Alistair Swiped pretending to be my mom so he can steal my ideas, I get mad all over again. "That guy is no good!" I yell.

"I agree," Manny says. "And a thief!"

"Someone should put his company out of business once and for all, so he'll stop ripping off other companies! And the poor kids who buy his terrible products!"

"Well, we're someone. Maybe *we* should put Swiped out of business!"

"Yeah!" I agree. Then I stop and think. "How?"

Manny thinks for a minute too. "Well," he says, "we've already gotten the ball rolling. He seems interested in Stench Quench."

I smile. "Yeah. Stench Quench may be the perfect way to stop Swiped. We just have to keep him interested. . . ."

Chapter Five

Turning a Nibble into a Bite

I WANT TO WRITE BACK TO ALISTAIR SWIPED RIGHT away, but Manny doesn't think that's a good idea. "Do you often write back quickly?"

"I don't know. Sometimes. But probably not. I write her, like, once or twice a day."

"And when you write to her twice in one day, do you write the e-mails back-to-back, or is it more like one e-mail in the morning and another e-mail in the evening?"

"I guess it's more like one morning e-mail and one night e-mail."

"Then we should wait. We don't want to

make Swiped suspicious in any way."

That makes sense, but it's hard to wait. I'd like to get revenge right away. I guess my face shows that I'm feeling impatient. Manny says he can read my face like a spreadsheet.

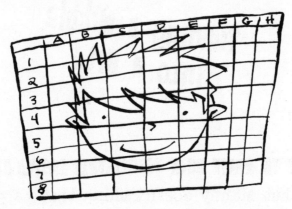

"Look, we got a nibble. But we want a bite, so we can hook this stinking fish," he says.

"Since when do you know anything about fishing?"

"Hey, I've been fishing!"

"How many times?"

"Once. With my uncle Jim. But it only takes one fishing trip to learn about nibbles and bites and hooks. You learn all that in, like, the first two minutes."

I smile, picturing Manny in a boat, fishing. I see him with a fishing pole in one hand and his phone in the other, checking sales figures while the fish steal all his bait.

"Okay, Mr. Fisherman," I say. "We'll put some really good bait on the hook and get Alistair Swiped to take a huge bite. Then we'll reel him in!"

"Great," Manny says. "We'll write back tomorrow."

The next day after school I head past the office to Manny's back door. His dad lets me in.

"Hi, Billy," he says. "How's business?"

"Good," I say automatically. When people first asked me how my business was doing, I used to give them long, detailed answers until I realized they didn't want long, detailed answers. I was just so excited about our new company that I liked talking about it. Now I mostly just say "good." (I'm still excited about it, though.)

"Not working in the office this afternoon?"

he asks. "Is everything okay out there? If there are any leaks, I'll be glad to fix them!"

Mr. Reyes teaches history, and when he's not working he enjoys trying to fix things around the house. Unfortunately, he's about as good a handyman as my dad is a chef. Manny still talks about the Kitchen Sink Disaster from two years ago. His dad tried installing a garbage disposal himself. We're still not sure how he did it, but he made it so when you turned on the faucet, garbage came out instead of water.

"No, everything's fine," I answer. "Manny and I just need to do something on the old computer in his room."

Mr. Reyes smiles. "Yes, I saw you two had set up that antique. I think that was the first computer we got for Manny. He was so excited. We thought he wanted to play computer games, but it turned out he wanted to make a spreadsheet of our household expenses!" He laughs.

I say good-bye to Mr. Reyes and head upstairs. Manny thinks we should keep corresponding with Alistair Swiped from his old computer, just to be safe, since that's the one that has the special spy software on it that my mom sent us.

"Ready to write?" Manny asks. "This baby's all fired up and ready to go!" he adds proudly.

"Ready!" I say, lacing my fingers together and stretching them out in front of me. "Are you sure you don't want to write this time?"

Manny shakes his head. "Definitely not. The e-mails have to stay consistent."

"All right, then," I say, sitting down in front of the computer. "Watch your back, Shakespeare, 'cause here I come." Manny's already opened a new e-mail document. I just have to type. I think for a second and then start writing. . . .

Hi, Mom,
    Had a good day at school today. Even the food in the school cafeteria was good!

"He's not going to believe that!" Manny jokes. "Pretty sure Swiped has never eaten in our cafeteria, so I think it should be okay."

"Let's get right to the stuff about Stench Quench," Manny suggests. "That's all this old thief is really interested in anyway."

"You got it!"

It wasn't easy concentrating on my studies. I'm so excited about Stench Quench! I know this is going to be a million-dollar idea. No, a BILLION-dollar idea!

"Too much?" I ask after I type that.

Manny considers it. "No, I don't think so. Swiped seems really greedy. It's good to tell him Stench Quench is a billion-dollar idea."

"Okay, how about a trillion-dollar idea?"

"Too much."

I know it sounds weird saying that kids will love a really gross drink. But kids love buying gross stuff, and grossing each other out.

"Do you think I should mention Mike Stevenson and his booger collection?" I ask.

"No way. We want to reel Swiped in, not gross him out."

Plus kids love to brag. It's like proving you're brave. "I bought a really gross drink! And I DRANK it! I'm braver than you are!"

"That's really good," Manny says. "Now I think you should put in the stuff about market research that we talked about."

"I'm not sure about this part," I say. "We haven't actually *done* any market research!"

"Yeah, but Swiped doesn't know that!"

"Okay, okay . . ."

Manny and I are doing some market research, and the results are really exciting! They show that kids LOVE the idea of Stench Quench! And they want to buy lots of it right away!

Manny rubs his face, thinking. "Maybe that's enough. We're just trying to bait the hook, not fill the boat with worms."

"Great. I'll wrap it up."

Now that I've told you more about Stench Quench, I can't wait to get back to work on perfecting the formula!
　　Love, Billy

"When did you fall in love with Swiped?" Manny teases. "And what made you love him? Was it the stealing or the spying? Or both?"

"Ha-ha," I say as I click send. "So what do you think? Do you think he'll go for it?"

Manny shrugs. "Who knows? I hope so. All we can do is wait to hear back from him and see what he says."

We don't have to wait long.

We were starting to leave the room, thinking we had time to go downstairs to the kitchen and grab a snack, when we heard the **DING!** of a new e-mail! We turn around and rush back to our chairs. This time I win the battle for the mouse and click on the new e-mail.

Hi, honey,

"Don't you just hate it when Alistair Swiped calls you 'honey?'" Manny asks, smiling.

"I'm so happy he wrote back that I don't care what he calls me," I say.

My work is going just fine. Glad to hear that you're so excited about your new idea for Stench Quench. And thanks for telling me more about it. I'm really busy, so I'll have to keep this note super short, but I'm curious about your market research.

"Uh-oh . . . ," Manny says.

I'd love to see the results of your research. I'm just so proud of the work you do that I'd love to be able to share it with my fellow employees here at work.

"That's pretty lame," I say.

"What is?"

"The 'I'd love to show your stuff to my colleagues' angle," I explain. "My real mom knows we keep our new inventions secret, especially in the early stages, so she'd never ask if she could show some of our research results to the people she works with."

> Gotta go! Love you so much! Love to your father and sister!
>
> Mom

"Well, it's nice to know that Alistair Swiped loves you back," Manny says, trying to keep the smile out of his voice.

"Yes, that is nice," I say, playing along. "So, what are we going to do about this market research?"

"I don't know," Manny says, getting up and wandering over to one of the chessboards. He moves a piece, and mutters, "Check." Then he looks back at me. "But whatever we do, we'd better do it fast. The longer we take, the more suspicious Swiped will become."

And then, just like that, it comes to me.

"I have an idea," I say.

I stand outside Emily's bedroom. The closed door has a sign on it: PLEASE KNOCK. ESPECIALLY YOU. GENIUS.

I knock. Gently. I've been warned many times about "pounding on the door like some kind of VIKING INVADER." *Knock, knock.*
Nothing.

The problem with knocking gently on Emily's door is that when she's in her bedroom, she almost always wears headphones so she can listen to music. Mostly British pop singers, lately. I don't know if she's listening to the music to improve her accent, or if the accent came after she started liking British music. It's hard to get inside her brain. And really, who would want to?

I try knocking a little louder. *Knock, knock!*

"WHO IS IT?" Emily yells from inside. From how loud she yells, I'm guessing she's still got her headphones on. She even yells in a British accent.

"It's me!" I say. "Your brother! Billy!"

"GO AWAY, GENIUS!" she shouts.

Silence. I'm guessing she's flopped down on her bed, listening to music and texting her friends and playing a game and reading an article about fashion, all at the same time.

Now I'm getting annoyed. To heck with her sign. I pound on the door. **KNOCK! KNOCK!**

Suddenly the door whips open. I don't even know how she got across her room that fast to open it. "WHAT DID I SAY ABOUT POUNDING ON MY DOOR?" she yells in her best British accent. Her headphones hang around her neck.

I decide to ignore her loud question. "
Em!" I say cheerfully. "Pip-pip! Cheerio! To
the mornin' to ya!"

She narrows her eyes. "It's afternoon," s
says in a low, murderous voice. "Almost ev
ning. What do you want?"

"I just need a tiny little favor." Before I ca
explain, she starts to close her door on me.

"Forget it," she says.

I stick my foot in the doorway to stop the
door from closing all the way. This is dangerous, since Emily has been known to stomp on
my foot, but I really need this favor.

"Actually, it's not for me," I say quickly.
"It's for Sure Things, Inc., and as the company's
vice president in charge of Next Big Thing
development, surely you want to help out."

Not too long ago, Manny and I hired Emily
to help wade through all the suggestions for
inventions that came in on our Next Big Thing
website. She'd insisted on being given a title
I'd actually forgotten what her title was. I ha
to look it up before I knocked on her door.

When I mention her title, Emily looks slightly less irritated. "Only if I'm paid," she says. Emily likes money.

"Okay," I agree, pretending to think it over, even though I knew she'd ask for money. "You'll be paid. And we need you to get some of your friends to help."

"They'll want to be paid too," she says.

"Fine," I say. "If you could get three or four of your friends to come over and help, that'd be great. Thanks."

I start to leave. Then I remember something and turn back. "Oh, and for this job, you'll have to lose the accent."

"What accent?" Emily asks in her British accent.

A couple days later I'm in the kitchen, pouring fruit juice into the blender. I'm following my mom's old recipe for fruit punch. (*Not* my dad's recipe. When he saw that I was mixing up fruit punch in the blender, he offered to show me how to make one of his kale and cabbage

smoothies, "chock-full of vitamins and anti-oxidants!")

I punch the button. **WHIRRRR!** I pour a little of the punch in a glass and taste it. It's really good. Now I just have to make it look awful.

On the counter there's a bag with food coloring in it. I pull out yellow, green, and blue. I pull off the tops and squeeze drops of food coloring into the fruit punch, combining the different colors until the punch looks like brownish, greenish sludge. Perfect.

My dad walks back into the kitchen. "How's the punch coming along?" he asks cheerfully. Then he sees what I've made. "Hey, you decided to use my recipe after all!"

A little later I'm in the backyard with the repulsive-looking punch, a video camera, Emily, and five of her friends—Maggie, Emma, Willa, Lauren, and Jody. (When word got out that they'd be paid for this, Emily had no trouble at all getting five friends to participate, even though I'd only asked for three or four.)

"Okay," I say. "It's really simple. All you have to do is drink this punch and pretend you love it." I gesture toward the muck in the pitcher I've placed on our picnic table.

"Drink that?!" Lauren says. "No way!"

"What is this? Some kind of stupid prank?" Willa asked, folding her arms across her chest.

"It tastes good," I explain. "It just *looks* bad because I put food coloring in it. Here, I'll show you." I pour myself a little glass and drink it. "See? It's fine."

Jody steps forward. "I'll try it," she says bravely. "How bad can it be?" I pour her a glass. She takes a tiny sip, then smiles. "It's good! Like fruit punch!"

"That's because it *is* fruit punch," I say. "But for the video, you're going to pretend it's something called Stench Quench. You're also going to pretend it smells and tastes terrible, but that you love how gross it is."

"Let me get this straight," Maggie says. "That's actually fruit punch. It looks horrible, but it tastes good. We're going to pretend it smells awful and tastes awful. And we love that because we love gross things."

"Exactly!" I say, delighted that Maggie's got it all figured out. I think I remember Emily saying that Maggie is her smartest friend.

"So we're pretending to be crazy people?" Willa asks.

"No, you're just normal kids who like gross stuff," I explain.

"You were right," I overhear Emma whisper to Emily. "Your brother's really weird."

"Just think about all the nail polish we can buy after we get paid," Emily reassures her.

I shoot several takes, and the girls get more and more into pretending that they love Stench Quench. "IT'S SO GROSS, IT'S GOOD!" Maggie says right into the camera.

In a couple of takes, Emily forgets that she's not supposed to use her British accent. When I say we have to do those over, she says "Why? Couldn't this be an international group?"

"Ooh, I want to be French!" Emma says. "Zis ees zee grossest zing I ever tasted!"

I convince them to just talk like themselves without any accents, and we do another take. I'm starting to worry that I didn't make enough Stench Quench.

In one take, Emily takes a sip and pretends the Stench Quench is so great that she faints. She lies in the grass for a second. "You can get up," I tell her. "I'm not sure we can use a version where the drink makes you pass out."

"The problem with you," Emily says, "is that you've got no imagination."

We finish with a shot where the girls scream like they've won the lottery. "WHERE CAN WE BUY STENCH QUENCH?"

"That's it!" I say. "Great job! We're done!"

In the office Manny and I use video-editing software to cut the different takes together into a single video. "Not too smooth," I say as Manny trims a few more seconds out of it. "We want this to look like a video of a marketing research test, not a TV commercial."

When the video's ready, we practically run with it up to Manny's bedroom. We can't wait to send it to Alistair Swiped. "I just hope that old computer's capable of sending a video," I say. "We may have to shovel some extra coal into its engine."

"I checked the requirements for sending video," Manny says as we clamber up the stairs. "It should be able to do it . . . slowly."

He's right about the "slowly" part. It seems as though it takes forever for the video to load onto the old computer's hard drive. Then I write an e-mail to go with the video.

Hi, Mom,

Just a quick note to say I'm sending you a recent video of a Stench Quench test-marketing session. It went well, as you'll see! All the sessions have gone great. Just thought you might enjoy seeing this one.

Love, Billy

"Oh no," Manny says, looking worried.

"What's the matter?" I ask. "Did I misspell something?"

"I just thought what if he recognizes Emily?"

"How would he recognize her? It's not like she's famous or anything?"

"She was on *Better Than Sleeping!* with you!"

He's right. I went on the late-night talk show *Better Than Sleeping!* to demonstrate the All Ball. At the end of my part of the show, the host, Chris Fernell, brought Manny, my dad, and Emily out onto the stage.

"That was just at the very end," I protest. "He probably didn't see that."

"*Probably,*" Manny repeats ominously. "She was also with you on *Wake Up, America!*"

He is right about that, too. When I went on the talk show to promote the Sibling Silencer, I demonstrated how it worked on Emily.

"If Swiped went through all the trouble to make up a fake e-mail address for your mom and e-mail you with it," Manny continues, "why wouldn't he make sure he recorded every one of your appearances on national television talking about your inventions?"

It's a really good point. I can't believe

I didn't think of this when I decided to put Emily in the phony test-marketing video. "I don't think we have time to reshoot the video," I say. "Swiped might get suspicious if we take too long to send him any proof that kids like gross stuff."

Manny gets up and starts pacing around. He says it helps him think. I think he's just burning off nervous energy. "Could we re-edit the video to cut out Emily?"

I shake my head. "I don't think so. She's right in the center of just about every shot. Emily likes being on camera."

"Maybe," Manny says, still pacing, "I could put a circle over her face, and we could explain that after we did the testing, one of the participants refused to let us show her face on video."

"Why?"

"Um, because she's in the Witness Protection Program?"

"I don't know. . . ."

Then I get an idea. "How about this?" I say, turning back to the computer keyboard.

P.S. One of the test participants may look a little familiar! Yes, that's Emily. She insisted on taking part in one of our marketing tests. (You know how she loves to be on camera.) That's why I'm sending you this particular video out of the dozens of Stench Quench test videos we've made. I knew you'd love seeing Emily again when you're so far away.

"Okay?" I ask.

Manny thinks a long time. Finally, he says, "Yeah. I think that's okay. It's believable that Emily might do that."

"Totally believable."

"All right," Manny says. "Let's send it."

It takes the computer quite a while, but finally a box pops up saying, "Message sent."

"I just hope Swiped takes the bait," Manny says.

"I bet he will," I say, trying to sound confident. "Taking stuff is his favorite hobby."

Chapter Six

Just Sleep On It

THAT NIGHT IN MY ROOM, AFTER I FINISH MY homework, I check my e-mail to see if there's anything from Alistair Swiped. I know I'm not supposed to *open* his e-mails on my bedroom computer, but I'm pretty sure it's safe to see if there's one in my in-box.

Nothing.

I hope Emily appearing in the video didn't ruin everything. Maybe I shouldn't have sent that video. Maybe I should have taken the time to reshoot the whole thing without Emily in it.

I decide to write an e-mail to my *real* mom.

When I type in the e-mail address, I triple-check to make sure I'm sending it to Mom and not to Alistair Swiped.

Hi, Mom,

We sure do miss you around here. Can't wait till your work lets you come back home. We'll all be so happy to see you. Philo might wag his tail right off.

Thanks again for your help with the corporate spy. We know who he is—he's the head of a rival company. And he's terrible— he steals ideas and then sells crummy products to kids. Manny and I decided that we want to put him out of business for good. So we e-mailed him, telling him we had this idea for something called Stench Quench. He acted interested and asked for more info. We sent him a video of some fake test marketing. We'll see if he takes that bait. . . .

I tell her some more stuff about what's going on at school and home and with Sure Things,

Inc. I think about asking her if she really is a spy, but then I think if she could tell me, she would. So either she isn't a spy, in which case I'll seem silly for suggesting it, or else she is a spy, but she can't tell me, so asking her will just make her feel bad about lying.

I decide not to ask.

Not long after I send the e-mail, my computer makes the chiming noise that tells me I've got a new e-mail.

Alistair Swiped?

No, it's my mom, writing back right away!

Hi, honey,

I'm always happy to hear from you and learn all about how you're doing.

I think you and Manny are doing an excellent job trapping the corporate spy. I'm impressed! I'm proud of you! (Of course, I'm always proud of you.) You and Manny would make great spies! That is, I imagine you would, based on what I see in the movies.

Good night, honey. Go to bed. But first
pet Philo for me.

Love, Mom (real one, not impostor)

Smiling, I pet Philo and get ready to go to
bed. But before I do, I get an idea.

Ever since I thought of the Stink Spectacular,
I've been working on coming up with the formula for it. That is, I've been working on it
whenever I could get a free moment from
schoolwork, the Stench Quench spy trap, walking Philo, and choking down Dad's meals.

I know Manny's not too enthusiastic about
this idea, but I love it, so I've been working
on it anyway. Without telling him. That part's
weird. I hate keeping secrets from Manny.

I've been able to make some drinks that
taste good. And I've been able to make some
drinks that smell terrible, like rotten eggs
mixed with moldy cucumbers. But I haven't
been able to come up with a drink that smells
awful but tastes wonderful. I've been getting
closer, but I still haven't nailed it.

I look up at the framed blueprints for the All Ball and the Sibling Silencer, which I came up with in my sleep. I have finished all of my big inventions in my sleep. I actually get up out of my bed and work on the inventions without ever waking up. In the morning, I find the finished blueprints on my desk. I know I do this, because Manny videotaped me finishing the Sibling Silencer blueprints in my sleep.

Some people sleepwalk. Some sleep-eat. I sleep-invent.

So far this has always happened when I wasn't expecting it to happen. I didn't even *know* yet that I was a sleep-inventor. It just happened.

But now that I know, can I *make* it happen? Or at least help it along somehow?

I'm getting pretty close on the Stink Spectacular formula. When I'm close is when I sleep-invent.

I open a drawer and dig out some blueprint paper. I lay it out neatly on my desk. On the left side of the paper, I carefully place a pen and a pencil. I'm right-handed, but when I sleep-invent I use my left hand. I know because I saw myself doing it in Manny's video.

MURF! MWURF! MOOF!

The muffled barks are coming from Philo. He's already asleep in his doggy bed next to my bed. He doesn't sleep-invent, but maybe he sleep-chases rabbits. Or cats. Or maybe even dragons—who knows what dogs dream about?

I look at the stuff laid out on my desk, satisfied. But is there something else I can do

to nudge my brain into a little sleep-inventing?

I open another desk drawer and find an index card. With a marker, I write "STINK SPECTACULAR" on the card. And even though this seems kind of silly, I put it under my pillow. I guess instead of leaving a tooth for the tooth fairy, I'm leaving a suggestion for my own brain.

Once all that's done, I lie down and fall asleep quickly.

I'm tied to a chair again. In an empty room. The walls go up so high that I can't see the ceiling.

The man dressed in gray enters the room. He stands in front of me, completely still, with his arms hanging at his sides. He's got his gray mask on, but there's a hole for his mouth.

He smiles, but it's not friendly. "Did you really think you could fool me?"

"Did you think you could fool *me*?" I ask defiantly. "I know who you are!"

"Stench Quench," he says slowly, as though it was a ridiculous combination of words.

"Absurd. You expected me to believe that?"

"Let me go," I say.

"Oh, I'll let you go," he says. "Up."

I'm confused. "Up?"

He nods slowly. "Up. Way up."

The man in gray walks over to the wall and flips a switch. Then he seems to get smaller.

But that's because I'm rising. He must have turned off the gravity in this room. Still tied to the chair, I'm floating.

Up.

Higher and higher and higher, until the man in gray is just a speck far below me. His quiet, mocking laughter floats up.

And then someone is licking my nose. . . .

The someone is Philo, naturally. Time to get up. Groggy, I roll out of bed and pull on some clothes, getting ready to take Philo outside.

But then I notice something.

The blueprint paper and the pencil and pen I put on my desk have moved. Suddenly I remember the card I put under my pillow! I pull it out. The word "'DONE!'" is scrawled across it. I try a quick experiment: I write "Done!" on the card with my left hand. It matches.

I hurry over to my desk and look at the blueprint paper. It's been written on!

I snatch up the papers and stare at them, a big grin spreading over my face. It's definitely a formula for the Stink Spectacular!

STINK SPECTACULAR

• • •

"The Stink Spectacular? I thought we agreed that was a bad idea," Manny says.

"Uh, no. *You* thought it was a bad idea. I thought it was a great idea."

We're in the office, playing foosball.

"So you went ahead and worked on it without telling me?" Manny says, twirling a line of miniature players.

"I don't have to tell you every time I'm working on inventing something! Sometimes I'm just thinking about an invention in my head. Do I have to tell you every time I start thinking about an invention?"

I realize that I sound like Emily. Not because I'm speaking with a British accent (because I'm not, of course) but because I sound defensive. But I'm getting kind of mad. I'm also feeling a little guilty about going ahead with an idea I knew Manny didn't like. After all, we're partners. I wonder if Emily has such complicated feelings going on all at the same time, and maybe that's why she's so obnoxious?

"We're partners!" Manny says as though he's reading my mind. "When it comes to the business of Sure Things, Inc., we have to tell each other everything!"

"Okay, I'm sorry," I say. And I mean it. "I should have told you. But last night I sleep-invented the formula! I think it's perfect!"

"Perfectly gross," Manny says.

"Yes, exactly! It's a million-dollar idea!"

Manny sighs. "You keep saying that, but I'm not sure I see it. I mean, I guess there might be a niche market for it."

"'Niche market?' Is that French?"

Manny makes his "I can't believe you don't know this" face.

"A niche market is a small, specialized market—a little group of specialized buyers with a particular, unusual taste for something. I think the niche market for Stink Spectacular is kids who are being bullied out of their drinks."

I think about that for a moment. "Okay, well, I think it's bigger than that. I think it's for kids who want to show they're brave enough to drink something that smells awful. Which is, like, almost every kid."

"It still sounds like a niche market to me. It might not have the big, general appeal of the All Ball and the Sibling Silencer. For our next invention, what about the Personal Force Field? Or the Dog Translator? Those are products with appeal for lots of people. I love those ideas!"

THWACK! THWOCK! The ball's really flying back and forth now, with both of us spinning the rods like mad, moving quickly from one end of the table to the other.

"I love those ideas too," I agree. "But I have a really good feeling about the Stink Spectacular. And now that I've sleep-invented the formula, I can't wait to try it out. All I have to do is get the ingredients, mix up a batch, and see if it works!"

Manny's face scrunches up so I can tell he's thinking hard about what I said. I'm hoping I managed to change his mind.

"I'm sorry, Billy," he says, not taking his

eye off the ball. "I just don't think I see it."

For a while we just play foosball. **THWACK!** **THWOCK!** And then, **CLONK!** The ball goes in the goal. On my end. Manny scores! He raises both fists above his head. I pretend to be mad he won, but Manny knows I'm only kidding. He usually beats me at foosball.

"You may have won the great foosball challenge, but I'm still going to make the Stink Spectacular," I say.

Manny just shrugs. He walks over to the free throw line, picks up the ball, and starts shooting free throws.

For the next several minutes, the only talking either of us does is Manny counting free throws. "One . . . two . . . three . . ."

Chapter Seven

The Fish Takes the Bait

LATER THAT DAY MANNY AND I ARE TAKING A BREAK from our Stink Spectacular debate when an e-mail arrives from Impostor Mom!

Manny's working at his computer in the office, checking sales figures. I'm working at my desk. It's almost like we've both been zapped with the Sibling Silencer. It's *that* quiet in the room.

I glance at my e-mail in-box and see there's new mail. "Swiped!" I yell, getting out of my chair.

"What about him?" Manny asks.

"He sent an e-mail!" Manny jumps up out of his chair and heads inside. I'm close behind.

We race through the kitchen. "Hi, Mom!" Manny yells. She gives a little wave, looking slightly confused. "Did you see more bugs out there?" She looks ready to spring into action.

"No!" Manny answers as he sprints up the stairs. "No bugs! Nothing to worry about!"

Unfortunately, the old computer isn't turned on. "It gets really hot if you leave it on," Manny explains. It takes forever to power up. We finally get through to my e-mail. I click on the message to open it.

Hi, honey,

Thanks so much for sending me that video! It was so nice to see Emily. She looked like she was having a great time. And so did the other girls. It's clear that they really do like the idea of the Stench Quench.

"I guess it was okay to have Emily in the video after all," Manny says.

"Looks like it," I say. "That's a relief."

I have to admit that I found it hard to believe kids would really want a drink that smells and tastes horrible. But now that I've seen the video, I guess they really do!

I'm curious about how you're going to make your Stench Quench. I worry a little that it might not be safe to drink. Would you mind sending your worried mother the recipe?

"Swiped wants the recipe!" I yell. My smile is as big as Manny's.

"He took the bait!" Manny says, holding up his hand for a high five. I gladly high-five him. This is great news!

Please promise me you won't try to make any Stench Quench until I've had a chance to run your recipe by some of the other researchers here. Maybe we'll make a test batch, just to be sure it's completely safe.

"He's obviously trying to keep you from making the Stench Quench before he does!" Manny says excitedly. "He wants to be the first one to sell Stench Quench! This is so great!"

Work's a little slow right now, so this would be a great time for us to test out your formula. But we're probably going to get swamped with work soon, so the sooner you send me your formula, the better.

Love to you and your father and Emily and the dog,

Mom

"He's so excited about the formula that he doesn't even bother to look up Philo's name in his records!" I point out. "We've completely got him! He's hooked!"

"Right!" Manny agrees. "Now all we have to do is send him the formula."

"True," I say. "But there's a problem."

"What's that?"

"We don't *have* a formula for Stench Quench! Remember?"

"Oh yeah," Manny says. "Well, we'll just have to come up with one. How hard can it be to make a recipe for a drink that smells and tastes terrible?"

I think about this for a moment. Then I grin. "I just happen to know an *expert* in things that smell and taste terrible!"

"You want me to do what?" Dad asks, not believing what he just heard me say.

"Show me how to make your kale and cabbage smoothie!" I say enthusiastically.

We're in his painting studio. It's a small wooden building he built himself in our backyard. The ceiling has skylights, so he can get lots of sunlight shining in to light up whatever he's painting. I always like coming into the studio. It smells like paint and wooden boards and stretched canvas. But I don't come in here too often, since Dad doesn't like being interrupted when he's painting.

"Well!" Dad says as he sticks his paintbrush into a jar of clear liquid with a bunch of other brushes spattered with paint. "That's great! But I must admit I'm surprised! I didn't know you were interested in cooking, Billy."

"Oh, I am!" I say, trying to sound as enthusiastic as possible. "Well, at least smoothies. I don't mean to interrupt you, though. I know you're busy. . . ."

"No, no! That's all right!" He wipes his hands off on a rag. "Any time's a good time for learning how to cook! I'll be happy to show you right now, if you like!"

"That'd be great!"

We go into the kitchen and Dad immediately opens the fridge and starts rummaging through the vegetable drawer. "Pretty sure I've still got some kale and cabbage in here somewhere. . . ."

He places the leafy green vegetables on the counter, then reaches up into the cabinet above the stove and pulls down a few small bottles. "The secret ingredients," he tells me with a wink, "are the seasonings. I use a special blend of garlic powder, onion powder, and cumin. That's what makes this drink really special!"

As I watch, my dad carefully measures out the stinky spices and mixes them together in a bowl. "Now let's blend us up a couple of smoothies!" he exclaims.

I ask him to wait just a moment while I run up to my room to get my tablet so I can take notes and pictures. Dad is thrilled I'm taking such an interest in cooking, so he happily pauses.

For once, Emily has her bedroom door open. "What are you doing, genius?" she asks.

"Cooking with Dad," I explain.

She makes a face. "You're a loony!" she says in her British accent. I have to admit, her accent's getting better. I think maybe she's watching British TV shows online.

I'm back downstairs in no time. I make sure to carefully take note of all the ingredients Dad uses, and the exact measurements. Dad turns on the blender, and within moments we have a fresh batch of his kale and cabbage smoothies. It's a disgusting green color. He pours me a glass and one for himself. Then he raises his glass in a toast. "To your health!"

I take a sip, pretending to gulp down more than I'm actually drinking. "Delicious!" I manage to croak out.

"Glad you like it!" he says, beaming. "Any more questions on how it's made?"

I shake my head. "Nope. I think I've got it."

"Good! If you don't mind, I think I'll take my smoothie out to the studio. I'd like to get some more done while the light's still right."

"Sure!" I say. "Thanks, Dad!"

"Anytime! Maybe next you'd like to learn how to make my tuna-guava-lima-bean casserole!"

"Maybe!" I say. "I'm not sure my cooking skills are quite up to that yet, though."

Once he's gone, I add some more ingredients to the drink. Sure it's disgusting, but I think it could be worse. Both the smell and the taste could be even more repulsive. I only use things I find in the fridge, like red onions, stinky cheese, and maple syrup. The more I add, the harder it gets to try tasting it. I consider calling Emily down to the kitchen, but I don't think any amount of money would make her drink this sickening slop. Even she's not *that* greedy.

I keep careful notes on everything I add to the Stench Quench. I think it's ready, but I'm not absolutely sure. . . .

"WHAT IS THAT HORRIBLE SMELL?" Emily suddenly yells from her room, completely dropping her British accent.

That's it. I've got it!

I jump on my bike and zoom over to Manny's. He's got the ancient computer ready.

Hi, Mom!

Thanks so much for offering to test my Stench Quench recipe! I really appreciate it!

I have to admit that at first, I didn't want to wait for you to do the safety tests on my Stench Quench. I'm excited about the idea, and so is Manny, so we'd like to get our new product on the shelves as soon as possible.

But we do want the Stench Quench to be safe for kids to drink, so we decided to wait until you give us the results of your tests. I'm attaching the recipe to this e-mail. IT'S SUPER-DUPER TOP SECRET AND WE HAVE NOT HAD TIME TO FILE ANY PATENTS ON IT OR ANYTHING LIKE THAT! PLEASE DON'T LET THIS FALL INTO THE WRONG HANDS!

"Like Swiped's hands!" Manny jokes.

"Exactly. Hey, maybe I should say that in the e-mail!"

Manny considers it, then shakes his head. "No, I think that's too risky. We should pretend we've never even heard of Alistair Swiped. We don't want him to suspect we're onto him."

"Yeah, you're right. It'd be funny, though. We could say something like, 'that obnoxious, ugly, smelly thief, Alistair Swiped.'"

"That dumb, stinking baboon, Alistair Swiped!"

"That nauseating, loud-mouthed loony, Alistair Swiped!"

""LOONY?"" Manny asks. "Who says 'loony'?"

"My sister."

"Quick piece of advice: Don't pick up vocabulary words from your sister."

Reason #239 Manny is a great CFO: He gives really good advice.

"Let's see," I say. "Where was I? Oh yeah. . . ."

Manny and I will really be looking forward to hearing what your tests say. Hope

the results don't take too long to come back.

Miss you and love you,

Billy

I read over the e-mail to see if it's all right. Manny agrees it's good. I click send, and off it goes.

"When do you think Swiped will send us his safety-test results?" I ask jokingly.

"Oh, probably on the twelfth."

"The twelfth? Of what?"

"Of never."

I get up from the desk chair and stretch. "Well, I'm glad we're done with the Stench Quench. It's in Swiped's hands now. I can concentrate on making the Stink Spectacular."

"Or the Personal Force Field Belt. Or the Dog Translator. . . ."

I pretend not to hear him.

Later in the week I realize I actually feel grateful to Emily for her help in making the Stench Quench video. And feeling grateful to Emily is so unusual that I decide to thank her.

Her door's slightly open, so I stick my head in. "Emily, I just wanted to thank you for all your help with the—"

I stop talking when I realize she's not listening. She's crying and punching her pillow. Like many things Emily does, the crying and punching seem a little overdramatic.

"What's wrong, Em?"

"Get lost!"

I turn and start to leave, but she sits up and shoots her arm straight out. "Wait!" she cries. I notice that even though it sounded like she was crying, her face looks dry. "Maybe it would be good for my soul to unburden myself."

She says this in her British accent.

"Okay," I say. "Unburden away."

She starts to speak, but then stops, as though it's too painful for her to say out loud.

"What is it?" I ask. "Is someone trying to kill you? Is it a vampire? Are *you* a vampire?"

She sighs heavily. Then, with her lower lip trembling, she blurts out, "Dad won't let me wear makeup!"

THAT'S ALL?

My brain immediately says, *That's all?* but luckily I've gotten better at not saying everything my brain comes up with. "Really?" I ask. "That's . . . terrible." I'm guessing, based on how she's acting, that Emily thinks it's terrible.

Sniffing, she says, "Yes, it is. All my friends get to wear makeup. I'm fourteen years old! I'm sure Mom would let me wear it if she were here, but she's off doing her stupid research! So I have to live under Dad's tyranny!"

I've never thought of my dad as a tyrant before. Somehow he doesn't seem like much of a tyrant, painting pictures of animals in his studio and cooking meals for us. If he forced us to *eat* the meals, knowing we hated them, I guess that might be kind of tyrannical. But he thinks his food tastes great, so he thinks he's doing something nice for us. But maybe all tyrants believe they are doing the right thing?

"Dad told me that if I sneak wearing makeup one more time, I'll be grounded."

"That's, uh, terrible." I'm having trouble thinking of different words for Emily's makeup tragedy. Or should I say made-up tragedy?

"There's this huge party tomorrow, and if I can't wear makeup like every single one of my friends, I'll just *die!*" She throws herself back down on her bed with her face buried in the pillow. She resumes punching the pillow, even though it doesn't seem like the pillow's done anything wrong at all.

Emily drives me crazy most of the time, but I certainly don't want her to die. And I feel as though I owe her for the Stench Quench video. I mean, not only did *she* act in the video, drinking my gross-looking fruit punch, but she also got a bunch of her friends to be in it.

She starts making crying sounds again. I know this sounds weird, but I'm pretty sure she's crying in a British accent.

"Em," I say. "Em, listen. I've got an idea."

She immediately stops crying and sits up. "What is it? Some kind of FATHER FREEZER?"

"What? No! What's a Father Freezer? You want to put Dad in a freezer?!"

"No, it'd be kind of like the Sibling Silencer, only instead of silencing your sibling, it'd freeze your father. You could go out and do whatever you want, and then when you came back you'd unfreeze your father, and he'd be fine, but he'd never know he was frozen or that you were at a party wearing makeup."

She's clearly given this some thought.

"Um, no, my idea isn't a Father Freezer. It's much less . . . diabolical. I think I could probably make my idea into a real thing for you in a couple of days."

She frowned. "That's no good. The party's tomorrow! If you're going to help me, you'll have to hurry. Go on! Get out of here! I'm sick of looking at you anyway!"

I guess it's nice to help my sister. But she doesn't make it easy.

Chapter Eight

Making Up Makeup

IT'S LATE FRIDAY NIGHT. I'VE SPENT EVERY SECOND since Emily kicked me out of her room learning about makeup. It's like makeup is this whole world I never knew existed. Thank goodness for the Internet.

I've got kind of a minilaboratory in a corner of my bedroom with a lot of chemicals and other stuff I can use for experiments. But I need even more chemicals, and other compounds that go into makeup. Down in the basement, I find old chemistry sets of mine and raid them. I even ride my bike to this

chemical supply store on the edge of town to pick up a few things. They know me there. "Hi, Billy!" they call out when I walk in the door. "How's the invention business?"

So now it's really late. Luckily, since it's Friday, I don't have to get up early tomorrow. I've made some progress on my idea, but there's still a pretty good distance left to go before I arrive at the thing I have in mind for Emily.

Should I keep working? I yawn so wide I think my mouth might split open. If I keep trying to work tonight, I'm probably going to pass out facedown in a bunch of chemicals.

Maybe I should forget the whole thing. Let her wait until she's sixteen to start wearing makeup, or whatever age Dad'll let her.

But she is my sister. And it would be nice.

How? There just isn't enough time.

Then I get an idea. I open one of my desk drawers and get out blueprint paper. I set the paper on top of the desk with pens and pencils. I find an index card and write "DISAPPEARING MAKEUP" on it.

That's my idea. Makeup that disappears after you apply it, only to reappear after you've left the house and passed Dad-inspection.

The question is, am I close enough with the formula to sleep-invent it?

I don't want to overdo it with the index cards under my pillow. It seems like if I stick a card under there every single night, I'll run out of sleep-invention power or something.

But since I really have no idea how my sleep-inventing works, I don't know how often is too often. I decide it's worth a shot.

I stick the card under my pillow, pat Philo on the head, and lie down in bed.

But before I fall asleep, I have another idea. I get up and turn on the little video camera on my computer, aiming it so it records most of my bedroom. I leave a small light on.

Will I be able to fall asleep with this light on? Yes, almost immediately.

I'm back in the empty room. But this time I'm not tied to a chair.

I'm sitting in front of a makeup mirror, staring at my reflection. There are all kinds of makeup on the counter in front of me, things I never knew existed—base, blush, eyeliner, eye shadow, mascara, lipstick, lip liner. . . .

My reflection starts to move. It turns blurry. And then it turns into the man dressed all in gray. This time he isn't wearing a mask. His face is gaunt and unfriendly.

I stare at him. He stares back at me. Then he frowns.

"What is all this?" he asks in his low voice.

"All what?" I ask.

"All this . . . makeup!"

"Just an invention I'm working on."

He looks confused. "What do *you* know about makeup?"

"Oh, I know plenty," I brag.

"Really?" he asks. He reaches out of the mirror and picks up a small container. He holds it up for me to see. "What's this?"

"That," I say confidently, "is lip liner."

"Wrong!" he says as he unscrews the top. He pulls a small brush out of the container. "Everyone knows that this is nose makeup."

"Nose makeup? There's no such thing!"

"There is now!" he says as he starts brushing wet makeup onto the tip of my nose. . . .

"Philo! Enough! Enough licking!"

It's Saturday morning. Too early to get up yet, but Philo doesn't know that, so he's licking my nose, waking me up. I gently push him away and get out of bed.

I feel really sleepy. Really, really tired . . .

But then I see the blueprints on my desk, and suddenly I'm wide-awake!

I hurry over to look at them. They're the formula for making Disappearing Makeup!

Sitting at my desk, I click on my webcam

video. At first I'm just sleeping. But when I fast-forward, I see myself get up out of bed, walk to my desk, sit down, and write with my left hand.

I pause the video and check my minilab desk. I find prototype makeup—everything Emily needs! It's not perfect yet—some of the colors are pretty weird—but it's a good start.

No wonder I felt so tired when I first got up. I must have been working most of the night!

Still, there's a lot more work to be done. I've got to refine this makeup, test it, and have it ready for Emily before her party tonight.

Just before lunch, I'm ready. I gather everything I've made and go down the hall to Emily's room. The door's closed. I knock. Gently.

"Enter!" she commands in her British accent.

I open the door and go in. Emily's lying across her bed on her stomach, looking absolutely miserable. "I have no life," she says. "I can't wear makeup, so I can't go to the party tonight. My social life is over."

I hand her the makeup. "Here. Try this."

She looks disgusted. "I thought you were supposed to be smart. I told you, Dad won't let me wear makeup! I'll be grounded!"

"This isn't ordinary makeup," I explain. "It's Disappearing Makeup."

Emily picks up the lipstick. "Disappearing Makeup? What's the point of that? If it disappears, you might as well not be wearing any makeup at all!"

"It disappears, but it comes back. When you put it on, it's triggered by the heat and energy from your skin. Within five minutes, it disappears. But then five minutes later, it reappears! And it lasts for hours, until it finally disappears from your face for good!"

Emily takes in what I'm saying. She starts to look a little less miserable.

"So," I continue, "here's what you do. About five minutes before you're going to leave for the party, you put on the makeup. Five minutes later, it's disappeared. You go show your face to Dad, who smiles and says, 'That's my beautiful clean-faced girl! Have fun at the party!' You hurry out the door, and within five minutes, you're all made up for the party. You go to the party, dazzle everyone, and come home completely clean-faced for Dad's late-night inspection. Simple!"

Emily gets it. She smiles. In fact, she's so thrilled, she gives me a big hug! "Thank you, Billy! This is wonderful!"

I pull away. Ew!

She opens the eye shadow and inspects it. "Although this isn't exactly the shade I like. Can you make me a soft bronze?"

Chapter Nine

What's Swiped Up To, Anyway?

AFTER CHOKING DOWN SOME OF DAD'S LUNCH, I TAKE
Philo and go over to the office. As we walk in,
Manny sinks a free throw and says, "Eighteen."

"Wow! Eighteen! That's really good," I say.

"Thanks," Manny says modestly. "My cur-
rent goal is twenty-five." The gadget that
automatically returns the ball arrived in the
mail yesterday.

It's still kind of weird between Manny and
me. I'm working on the Stink Spectacular, but
not around Manny because I know he hasn't
warmed up to the idea. I think he knows I'm

working on it, though, because he doesn't ask me anything about when our next product will be coming out. He works on the marketing and sales of the All Ball and the Sibling Silencer. And he shoots free throws.

"I wonder what's going on with Swiped," I say. "Impostor Mom hasn't written me any more e-mails."

"Maybe that's because he got what he wants," Manny suggests. "Once we sent him the recipe, he had what he needed."

"I just wish I knew what he's up to. It *seems* like he took the bait, since he asked us for the Stench Quench recipe, but we don't know what he's doing with it. Once he saw the recipe, he may have rejected the idea. Or he may have figured out that the whole thing was a trap."

Manny sets down the All Ball and goes over to his desk. He sits down and starts typing. "Let's see if there's any news about what Swiped is up to."

He clicks on an article, reads a little, and says, "AHA! JACKPOT!"

"What is it?" I ask.

"Listen to this! 'Alistair Swiped of Swiped Stuff, Inc. to introduce new product on prime-time TV!'"

"*What?* All right!"

Manny keeps reading. "Alistair Swiped, the CEO of Swiped Stuff, Inc. is betting big on his new product. He's bought seriously expensive television time to introduce the mystery product tonight."

"*Tonight?* That was quick!"

Manny turns and faces me. "Yeah, well, once he got the recipe, it wouldn't take him that long to whip up a batch of Stench Quench. You did it in your kitchen in, what, twenty minutes?"

"I don't think it even took that long."

"So if you're Swiped and you have the resources of your whole company behind you, you could probably get a bunch of Stench Quench made really quickly! I'll see if anyone knows what the product is," Manny says, turning back to his computer. He searches, and comes up with tons of articles. Lots of business websites have articles on Swiped's bold move. They say that Swiped has even hired TV personality Chris Fernell, the host of the late-night talk show *Better Than Sleeping!*, to interview celebrities, getting their reactions to his exciting new product. But no one knows what the product is. Alistair Swiped has managed to keep that a secret, despite the best efforts of every business reporter to find out.

"Do you really think his new product is going to be Stench Quench?" I ask. "That would be so incredibly awesome!"

"And sweet revenge! Because the product would be sure to fail. Nobody wants a drink that smells awful," Manny says gleefully.

This seems like a pretty obvious criticism of the Stink Spectacular, but I let it go. "Wanna sleep over at my house tonight and watch Swiped's big show?"

"Sure," Manny says. "I wouldn't miss it."

I'm a little worried that it might be kind of awkward having Manny spend the night while we're disagreeing about the Stink Spectacular. But I have a plan.

After dinner I'm going to offer Manny an early version of the Stink Spectacular to show him how delicious it is. I'm pretty sure he'll love it, and agree that we should produce it. But if he doesn't, we won't. I respect his opinions. That's why he's my chief financial officer.

Once Dad has finished his painting and comes into the kitchen to fix dinner, we wander in there to find out what he's making. I figure it's better to have a little time to get used to the smell of Dad's dinner instead of just having his latest creation sprung on you. Like a deadly tiger.

Dad's at the counter, mixing something in a bowl. "What's for dinner, Dad?" I bravely ask.

"Well, it's pretty warm today, so I thought maybe I'd grill."

That doesn't sound so bad.

"W-what are you grilling?" Manny asks nervously. He's eaten at our house before. Though he usually does his best to avoid it.

"Cheeseburgers."

CHEESEBURGERS?! Something normal? And potentially delicious?

"I thought maybe some simple, old-fashioned cheeseburgers might taste good tonight," he continues. "I don't have to cook gourmet creations *every* night. Besides, I've noticed a fair amount of food being left on plates lately." He winks at me.

Cheeseburgers! Things are looking up!

Emily comes into the kitchen, which is unusual, since she usually avoids the kitchen when Dad's cooking. She's got her sulky face on. If there were contests for sulking, Emily's room would be full of trophies.

"Well, the party tonight is going to be completely humiliating, since I'll be the only one not wearing makeup," she says.

SULKY GIRL
CHAMPIONSHIPS
1ST PLACE

She turns so that I can see her face but my father can't. She shoots me a quick smile. It's all an act. I think she's laying it on a bit thick.

But my father buys it. "Now, honey," he says reassuringly, "we've discussed this. Right now you're too young for makeup. But don't worry. We'll revisit the whole makeup issue. When you're sixteen."

"By then it'll be too late! I'll already be a social outcast!" She stomps out of the room dramatically, flashing me another smile.

Chapter Ten

The Next Big Thing

AMAZINGLY, THE CHEESEBURGERS ARE DELICIOUS.
Dad didn't even put one little shred of kale in
them. For once Philo hangs around while we
eat. I toss him a bite. *Chomp!*

As we leave the dining room, Manny says,
"I think those were the best cheeseburgers I
ever had. Are you sure your dad made them?"

"Let's have something else delicious!" I say,
pretending it just occurred to me.

"Dessert?" Manny asks eagerly.

"Sort of," I say. "Let's go upstairs and try
some Stink Spectacular!"

Manny's face falls. "You've made the Stink Spectacular?"

"An early version," I say. "I'm still refining it, but it's good. Come on, give it a try."

Manny hesitates. Then he nods his head slowly. "Okay," he says. "I'll try it."

We go up to my room and I get a plastic jug out of the minifridge. It's full of red liquid.

"It doesn't *look* bad," Manny says.

"I want the color to be appealing, since the smell is so bad."

As I take the lid off, Manny looks a little nervous. I pour two glasses and hand him one. He makes a face. "Yuck! Man, does this *stink!*"

"That's the idea," I say. "But wait till you taste it."

He lifts the glass to his mouth, squeezes his eyes shut, and takes a tiny sip.

"Well?" I ask.

Before Manny answers, Emily comes in. She's wearing the Disappearing Makeup. I don't know much about makeup, but it looks to me as though she's put on plenty.

"Well, what do you think?" she whispers.

"Is the party you're going to, like, a circus party or something?" Manny asks, puzzled.

"Circus party? No! Why?"

"Because you're wearing clown makeup," Manny says. He still has a long way to go before he's mastered talking to sisters.

"This is *not* clown makeup!" Emily hisses. "You obviously know nothing about makeup!"

"That's true," Manny admits.

"Eww," Emily says, wrinkling her nose. "What's that smell?"

"Stink Spectacular," I answer, raising my glass. "Want some?"

She rolls her eyes and sighs, as though this

is not even remotely worth an answer.

Suddenly Manny points at Emily. "Hey, the makeup looks better! Less clownlike!"

"That's because it's disappearing," I explain. As we watch, Emily's makeup fades away and completely disappears.

Emily looks at herself in the mirror. "Success! Gotta go!" She gives me a quick hug (I'm not sure I like the new hugging Emily) and rushes out to pass Dad's inspection before she goes with her friends to the big party.

"What was *that* all about?" Manny asks, completely baffled.

I feel a little embarrassed to admit that I've been using my inventing skills on makeup. On the other hand, I'm proud that my Disappearing Makeup works.

"Dad won't let Emily wear makeup, so I invented Disappearing Makeup. She puts it on, and after about five minutes it disappears. She shows her face to Dad and leaves for her party. In another five minutes, the makeup reappears and stays on for several hours. At the end of the night it disappears again, so Dad won't see it when she gets home from the party."

Manny just sits there, staring at me.

"It's really no big deal," I say, wondering if he's mad that I spent so much time on something for Emily instead of focusing on inventing something for Sure Things, Inc. "Just a little thing I made for Emily because she helped us out with the Stench Quench video."

"Disappearing Makeup," Manny finally says, nodding slowly. "That . . . is . . . BRILLIANT!"

"It is?"

"Absolutely! Do you have any idea how big the cosmetics industry is?"

"Um . . . no."

"It's huge! A multibillion-dollar business! And I'm pretty sure teenage girls are a big chunk of that business! And your product is revolutionary! There's never been anything like it!"

I shrug. "Thanks. Makeup's not really my thing, so I didn't think it was a big deal."

Manny is so excited he stands up and paces

around my room. "It may not be your thing, but it could be our next big thing! This is the product we've been waiting for!"

I trust Manny's instincts. If he says Disappearing Makeup is a Sure Thing, I believe him. After all, we're partners. We have to work together if Sure Things, Inc. is going to make it. Or keep making it.

I still like my idea for the Stink Spectacular. Actually, I love it. And I think kids would love it. But like I said, I trust Manny's instincts.

"I think we should try to put out Disappearing Makeup as soon as possible," Manny continues. "We're still getting a lot of attention because of the All Ball and the Sibling Silencer, so we should launch another product while people are paying attention to Sure Things, Inc. And we need some huge platform for the launch."

I'm confused. "We're going to build a huge platform? Out of wood? Like a pirate ship?"

Manny laughs. "You never, ever read the business journals I loan you, do you?"

"I tried. Once. Too boring."

"A platform is something you use to show off you new product, like the Internet or TV. Actually, the one good idea Swiped had was introducing his new product live on TV during prime time with lots of celebrities. He'll probably get millions of viewers."

"Speaking of the show, it's time!" I realize. We run downstairs to the living room.

Chapter Eleven

Showtime!

MANNY AND I SETTLE DOWN WITH MY DAD AND PHILO in the family room. "What is this that we're watching, anyway?" Dad asks.

"It's kind of a spy show," Manny says.

"Okay," Dad says. "I like spies."

Enough to marry one? I think. From the look on his face, Manny's thinking the same thing.

On the TV, a band plays some music, and Chris Fernell enters. The live studio audience applauds.

"Hello, everyone, and welcome to this very special television event! Tonight we're going to learn about an exciting new product from world-famous businessman Alistair Swiped!"

"World famous?" my dad asks. "Never heard of him."

"I know we're all waiting to find out what the new mystery product is, so let's bring it on out, okay?" Chris says enthusiastically.

The audience claps and cheers. A pretty woman wheels a cart out with cups, a bucket of ice, and a stack of cans on it.

"Do those cans say what I think they do?" Manny asks, excited.

"I think so!" I say, standing up and getting closer to our TV.

"Stench Quench!" we both yell at the same time. Philo barks, wanting to join in.

"Stench Quench?" Dad says. "What's that? I thought this was a spy show."

Chris Fernell picks up one of the cans and holds it out so the audience can see it. "Alistair Swiped's exciting new product is . . . STENCH QUENCH!"

There's some quiet, scattered applause, but

mostly the audience seems quite puzzled.

Chris Fernell moves to a couch. "I know, it's kind of a funny name. Let's bring out the inventor to explain it to us. Please welcome . . . ALISTAIR SWIPED!"

A tall, thin man with stringy hair enters from behind a curtain and gives a little wave to the audience. I realize he looks a little bit like the man dressed all in gray in my dreams. And the man in the picture we got from my mom's spy software. Wait, did I just call my mom a spy? I didn't mean that! Anyway, I never realized before now that the guy in my dreams is the same guy from the picture.

Alistair Swiped.

He sits down on the couch next to Chris Fernell. Chris says, "So, Alistair, tell us. What's the deal with Stench Quench?"

Swiped smiles, at least with his mouth. His eyes don't really look like they're smiling. "Well, Chris," he says, "first let me ask you something. Do you have children?"

Chris smiles a real smile. "Yes, I do. Two

beautiful children. Twins. A boy and a girl."

"Do they like gross things?"

Chris laughs. "Yes! They love gross stuff! You should see the things they bring into the house! If we go to the park, it's like they've got some kind of radar for grossness. They zoom right in on it! Next thing I know, it's on our kitchen table!" The audience laughs.

"Well, Stench Quench is perfect for them! Stench Quench is a new drink that tastes even worse than it smells!"

"Okay," Chris says, looking a little puzzled. "Should we try some?"

"I have an idea," Swiped says, trying to act as though this idea just occurred to him, even though it obviously was planned. "Why don't we let Dustin Peeler try some?"

The audience applauds, and Dustin Peeler enters through a curtain. Just last summer, he was the biggest pop star on the planet. But lately he's been getting into trouble, and he's not quite as popular as he was. That's probably why Swiped was able to hire him.

"Dustin Peeler . . . ," Dad says. "Doesn't Emily like him? Too bad she's missing this. Maybe I should record it."

"I don't think Emily really likes Dustin Peeler anymore, Dad," I say.

After greeting Chris Fernell and Alistair Swiped, Dustin pops open a can of Stench Quench. He's obviously repulsed by the smell. "Whew!" he says, waving his hand in front of his nose.

"Isn't that disgusting?" Swiped says. "Kids are gonna love it!"

Dustin holds the can in front of him, hesitating.

"Go ahead," Swiped urges him. "Taste it!"

"Okay," Dustin says. "Here goes."

He lifts the can to his lips and drinks. His eyes bulge. You can see he wants to spit it out immediately, but Swiped glares at him, and he swallows the Stench Quench.

"Well?" Chris Fernell asks.

"Excuse me!" Dustin blurts out. He jumps up from the couch and runs off the stage. From the wings, there's the unmistakable sound of someone throwing up.

Manny and I laugh. Dad's totally confused. "I really don't get this show at all."

But we keep watching, and it just gets better and better. Fernell and Swiped keep bringing out different celebrities and audience members and kids to try drinking the Stench Quench, but they all end up having the same reaction as Dustin Peeler.

Soon the audience is booing. "This is terrible!" one woman yells. "Stop making people drink that horrible stuff!"

Even Chris Fernell can't take it anymore.

"I don't care how much you're paying me, Swiped. This is just wrong. Stench Quench is a DISASTER!"

The audience applauds. Utterly humiliated, Alistair Swiped gets up and runs off the set.

To tell the truth, I feel a little sorry for him. On the other hand, he's a thief and a bad guy, so revenge is sweet.

Chris Fernell watches him go, and then checks his watch. "Well, this is a little awkward, folks. Swiped paid for half an hour of live television, and we've only used up eight minutes." Chris is a professional, so he doesn't look particularly nervous about having to fill twenty-two minutes of live television. "Let's see who else is backstage," he says, consulting a list. "Maybe there's still someone back there who hasn't been sickened by Stench Quench. Oh, here's one of my favorite baseball players, the shortstop for the Hyenas, Carl Bourette!"

I can't believe it. My favorite athlete of all time walks out through the curtain, smiling and waving. The audience goes nuts.

Carl sits on the couch with Chris. "You know," he says, "in all my years playing baseball, I've seen some real disasters, but this one takes the cake."

"You think my career will survive this?" Chris asks.

"Oh, I think so," Carl says. "But I don't know about that Swiped fellow."

"Dad," I say, "are you recording this?"

"Yeah," he says.

"Good, because this is the greatest thing I've ever seen on TV."

Carl's still talking about Alistair Swiped.

"Of course, inventing's a tough business. It might be even more competitive than professional baseball. I sure wouldn't want to try it."

Chris nods. "I agree. I think I'll stick to hosting a talk show. Compared to inventing, that's easy as pie."

"Speaking of inventors," Carl says, "you remember that kid, Billy Sure?"

WHAT?!

"Oh, absolutely," Chris says. "We had him on my show. You were on that night. We tossed around the All Ball."

"What is happening?" I say.

"Whatever it is, it's very, very good," Manny says, his eyes glued to the TV set. He's grinning.

"Now *there's* an inventor!" Carl says. "I wonder what he's up to?"

"Let's find out!" Chris says. He turns to the audience. "Should we call Billy Sure and ask him what he's up to?"

The audience applauds!

"Hey, Sarah!" Chris calls offstage to an assistant. "Do you still have Billy Sure's phone number from when he was on the show? Let's call him right now!"

The assistant walks onstage dialing a cell phone. She hands the phone to Chris.

Our phone rings!

"I can't believe this is happening!" I yell.

"Answer your phone!" Manny shouts.

I answer it. "Hello?"

"Hi, Billy!" Chris Fernell says. "I'm sitting here with an old pal of yours, Carl Bourette, and we were wondering if you've got any new inventions you'd like to tell us about!"

"I know," I manage to say. "I'm watching you on TV."

Chris laughs. "Keeping an eye on the competition, huh? Well, I don't think you have to worry about Alistair Swiped anymore. So, what are you working on?"

I try to tell him about Disappearing Makeup, but I realize I don't know what to say. I'm usually not really nervous when I have to talk about Sure Things, Inc. business, but this time I'm not prepared, and I've never really spent any time talking about makeup before. My mind goes completely blank.

"Ummm . . . Before I tell you about what we're working on, can Carl Bourette maybe tell us who his favorite baseball player is? I'm dying to know."

Carl immediately starts talking, and I figure I have about thirty seconds to come up with something to say about Disappearing Makeup. I try to line up a sales pitch in my head, but all I can think of is how Emily looked like a clown with all her makeup on. I look around the room frantically. Twenty seconds. Still nothing. Philo and my dad stare at me, and it feels like time has stopped. On the television, Carl Bourette wraps up whatever he was saying (I can't believe I missed his answer!) and I know I have about five seconds to come up with something. *Think!* I tell my brain. Then I notice Manny signaling for me to give him the phone. He whispers, "Trust me." And I do, of course. I hand him my phone.

Manny introduces himself and does this

amazing double pitch, perfectly describing Disappearing Makeup *and* Stink Spectacular! He even renames the Disappearing Makeup "DISAPPEARING REAPPEARING MAKEUP," which is a much better name. I'm so blown away by his perfect explanation of it (how does he know so much about the cosmetics industry offhand?) that I almost fall off my chair when he switches gears and starts talking about Stink Spectacular as well. The audience eats up everything he says.

Reason #732 Manny is my CFO: He's brilliant.

The time flies by, and Chris Fernell wraps up the show. "Well, that's all the time we have! Sorry about the start of our show, but wasn't it great hearing about Sure Things, Inc.'s new inventions, Disappearing Reappearing Makeup and Stink Spectacular?"

The audience cheers again.

I can't believe it.

Not only did we get sweet revenge on Alistair Swiped, but we also got to promote our newest product. Products, I should say!

"I can't believe you decided to talk about Stink Spectacular, too!" I say to Manny.

"I realized that right after Stench Quench bombed was the perfect time to introduce Stink Spectacular as a gag gift that tastes delicious."

"You think it's delicious?"

"Definitely! Let's have some more to celebrate!"

My dad just shakes his head. "That was the weirdest spy show I ever saw."

Chapter Twelve

Sure Things

MANNY AND I WORK REALLY HARD TO GET DISAPPEARING Reappearing Makeup and Stink Spectacular ready to sell as quickly as possible.

And after we launch them, sales take off!

I arrive at the office, fully expecting Manny to be glued to his computer, reviewing sales figures. But when I walk in, I'm surprised to see him standing at the free throw line. He launches the ball. *Swish!* He pumps his fist.

"FIFTY!"

"Fifty?" I say. "You just made fifty free throws in a row?!"

Manny nods, grinning.

"That's fantastic! Don't stop. Keep going!"

He shakes his head. "I hit my goal. I'll set a new goal, but for now, I walk away."

"I have something to show you," I say. I take a picture out of my backpack.

"What's this?" Manny asks.

"Disappearing Reappearing Makeup's new model."

"It's Emily! But what about your dad?"

I sit down at my desk and smile. "He talked to my mom, and she said Emily's old enough to wear makeup, so he's cool with it. So Emily gets to be in our ads."

"That's great!" Manny says.

We laugh. My computer goes **PING BONG BING!** It's a video chat request from my mom!

I click on "Answer With Video" and see her smiling face. She's dressed all in black.

"Hi, honey!" she says. "I wanted to congratulate you and Manny again on a great job of counter-espionage! I assume there have been no more e-mails from the spy?"

"Well, there was one," I say.

"Really?" she asks. "What did it say?"

"It said, 'You win. For now!'"

She shrugs. "Well, that doesn't sound too—"

Suddenly there's a commotion behind her. "Oops! Gotta go!" she says.

But before she signs off, I'm pretty sure I see her swing into action, fighting off what looks like a bunch of ninjas!

I sit there, stunned. Then I realize Manny's behind me. He saw the end of the call too.

"I'm telling you, dude," he says. "Your mom's definitely a spy!"

BILLY SURE

•KID ENTREPRENEUR•

AND THE CAT-DOG
TRANSLATOR

INVENTED BY LUKE SHARPE
DRAWINGS BY GRAHAM ROSS

"You want this, boy?" I ask, waving Philo's favorite chew toy at him.

Philo dashes over to where I'm sitting, and grabs one end of the toy in his teeth. He tugs hard, pulling me from my chair. I tumble to the rug, laughing. Letting go of my end of the toy, I put my arm around Philo and start to play-wrestle with him.

"What's going on down there!" shouts Emily, my sister, from upstairs. "Some of us have homework to do, y'know!"

"Just playing with Philo," I call back.

"Well, do it quietly!" she screams down.

I pick up Philo's chew toy and wave it over my head. "Go get it!" I shout.

Philo turns and dashes after the rope. He snatches it up in his mouth, then trots toward me, dropping it at my feet.

"Again?" I ask.

"Ruufff!" he replies.

Sometimes it's as if I can actually understand what Philo is saying.

"One more time." I toss the rope back over Philo's head. It bounces a couple of times, then disappears into the dining room.

Philo turns and chases after it, but then he doesn't come back.

"Get the toy, Philo!" I shout.

No Philo. No toy.

As I step into the dining room, I find the chew toy sitting on the floor, but Philo is all the way on the other side of the room.

"It's right here, boy," I say, pointing at it.

Philo paces back and forth across the floor on the far side of the dining room. He stops, sniffs under some furniture, then turns and walks back to the other side of the room, where he repeats this.

"Urrrr . . . yip-yip!" he says.

"What is it, boy?" I ask.

"Urrrr . . . yip-yip!" he repeats.

Now I really wish I could understand what Philo is saying. Things would be much easier. I could just give him what he wants and he'd be happy. And then I wouldn't spend so much time wondering what he's trying to say.